About the Author

NEWTON ('NEWT') ARTEMIS FIDO SCAMANDER was born in 1897. His interest in fabulous beasts was encouraged by his mother, who was an enthusiastic breeder of fancy Hippogriffs. Upon leaving Hogwarts School of Witchcraft and Wizardry, Mr Scamander joined the Ministry of Magic in the Department for the Regulation and Control of Magical Creatures. After two years at the Office for House-Elf Relocation, years he describes as 'tedious in the extreme', he was transferred to the Beast Division, where his prodigious knowledge of bizarre magical animals ensured his rapid promotion.

Although almost solely responsible for the creation of the Werewolf Register in 1947, he says he is proudest of the Ban on Experimental Breeding, passed in 1965, which effectively prevented the creation of new and untameable monsters within Britain. Mr Scamander's work with the Dragon Research and Restraint Bureau led to many research trips abroad, during which he collected information for his worldwide bestseller *Fantastic Beasts and Where to Find Them*.

Newt Scamander was awarded the Order of Merlin, Second Class, in 1979 in recognition of his services to the study of magical beasts, Magizoology. Now retired, he lives in Dorset with his wife Porpentina and their pet Kneazles: Hoppy, Milly and Mauler.

THE HARRY POTTER SERIES

In reading order:
Harry Potter and the Philosopher's Stone
Harry Potter and the Chamber of Secrets
Harry Potter and the Prisoner of Azkaban
Harry Potter and the Goblet of Fire
Harry Potter and the Order of the Phoenix
Harry Potter and the Half-Blood Prince
Harry Potter and the Deathly Hallows

Also available in Latin:
Harry Potter and the Philosopher's Stone
Harry Potter and the Chamber of Secrets

Also available in Welsh, Ancient Greek and Irish:
Harry Potter and the Philosopher's Stone

ILLUSTRATED EDITIONS

Illustrated by Jim Kay
Harry Potter and the Philosopher's Stone
Harry Potter and the Chamber of Secrets
Harry Potter and the Prisoner of Azkaban

COMPANION VOLUMES

Fantastic Beasts and Where to Find Them
Quidditch Through the Ages
(Published in aid of Comic Relief and Lumos)

The Tales of Beedle the Bard
(Published in aid of Lumos)

The three companion volumes also available as:
The Hogwarts Library
(Published in aid of Comic Relief and Lumos)

NEWT SCAMANDER

FANTASTIC BEASTS

AND WHERE TO FIND THEM

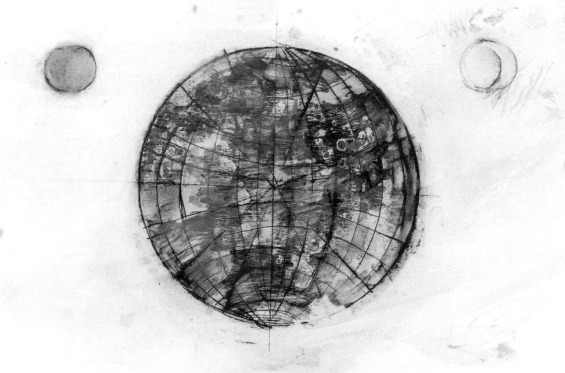

J.K. ROWLING

Illustrated by

OLIVIA LOMENECH GILL

BLOOMSBURY

LONDON OXFORD NEW YORK NEW DELHI SYDNEY

in association with

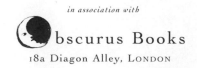

Obscurus Books

18a Diagon Alley, LONDON

For Gabhran, Elzéard and Arthos
O.L.G.

Bloomsbury Publishing, London, Oxford, New York, New Delhi and Sydney

First published in Great Britain in 2001 by Bloomsbury Publishing Plc

50 Bedford Square, London WC1B 3DP

www.bloomsbury.com

Bloomsbury is a registered trademark of Bloomsbury Publishing Plc

This edition published in 2017

Text copyright © J.K. Rowling 2001

Cover and interior illustrations by Olivia Lomenech Gill copyright © Bloomsbury Publishing Plc 2017

A CIP catalogue record of this book is available from the British Library

ISBN 978 1 4088 8526 0

1 3 5 7 9 10 8 6 4 2

Printed and bound in China

Comic Relief (UK) was set up in 1985 by a group of British comedians to raise funds for projects promoting social justice
and helping to tackle poverty. Monies from the worldwide sales of this book will go to help children and young people in
the UK and around the world, preparing them to be ready for the future – to be safe, healthy, educated and empowered.

Comic Relief (UK) is a registered charity: 326568 (England/Wales); SC039730 (Scotland).

Named after the light-giving spell in the Harry Potter books, Lumos was set up by
J.K. Rowling to end the use of orphanages and institutions for vulnerable children around the
world by 2050 and ensure all future generations of children can be raised in loving families.

Lumos is the operating name of Lumos Foundation, a company limited by guarantee
registered in England and Wales, number 5611912. Registered charity number 1112575.

With thanks to J.K. Rowling for creating this book and so generously giving all her royalties from it to Comic Relief and Lumos

Contents

ABOUT THE AUTHOR   i

FOREWORD BY THE AUTHOR   viii

INTRODUCTION

    ABOUT THIS BOOK   x

    WHAT IS A BEAST?   xi

    A BRIEF HISTORY OF MUGGLE AWARENESS   xiii
    OF FANTASTIC BEASTS

    MAGICAL BEASTS IN HIDING   xv

    WHY MAGIZOOLOGY MATTERS   xvii

MINISTRY OF MAGIC CLASSIFICATIONS   xviii

AN A-Z OF FANTASTIC BEASTS   1

LIST OF BEASTS   135

Foreword by the Author

IN 2001, A REPRINT of the first edition of my book *Fantastic Beasts and Where to Find Them* was made available to Muggle readers. The Ministry of Magic consented to this unprecedented release to raise money for Comic Relief, a well-respected Muggle charity. I was permitted to reissue the book only on condition that a disclaimer was included, assuring Muggle readers that it was a work of fiction. Professor Albus Dumbledore agreed to provide a foreword that met the case and we were both delighted that the book raised so much money for some of the world's most vulnerable people.

Following the declassification of certain secret documents kept at the Ministry of Magic, the wizarding world has recently learned a little more about the creation of *Fantastic Beasts and Where to Find Them*.

I am not yet in a position to tell the full story of my activities during the two decades that Gellert Grindelwald terrorised the wizarding world. As more documents become declassified over the coming years, I will be freer to speak openly about my role in that dark period in our history. For now, I shall confine myself to correcting a few of the more glaring inaccuracies in recent press reports.

In her recent biography *Man or Monster? The TRUTH About Newt Scamander*, Rita Skeeter states that I was never a Magizoologist, but a Dumbledore spy who used Magizoology as a 'cover' to infiltrate the Magical Congress of the United States of America (MACUSA) in 1926.

This, as anyone who lived through the 1920s will know, is an absurd claim. No undercover wizard would have chosen to pose as a Magizoologist in that period. An interest in magical beasts was considered dangerous and suspect, and taking a case full of such creatures into a major city was, in retrospect, a serious mistake.

I went to America to free a trafficked Thunderbird, which was quite risky enough, given that MACUSA had a curse-to-kill policy on all magical creatures at the time. I am proud to say that one year after my visit, President Seraphina Picquery instituted a Protective Order on Thunderbirds, an edict she would eventually extend to all magical creatures. (At President Picquery's request, I made no mention of the more important American magical creatures in the first edition of *Fantastic Beasts*, because she wished to deter wizarding sightseers. As the American wizarding community was subject to greater persecution at that time than their European counterparts, and given that I had inadvertently contributed to a serious breach of the International Statute of Secrecy in New York, I agreed. I have reinstated them in their rightful place in this new edition.)

It would take months to contradict every other wild assertion in Miss Skeeter's book. I shall simply add that, far from being 'the love rat who left Seraphina Picquery heartbroken', the President made it clear that if I didn't leave New York voluntarily and speedily, she would take drastic steps to eject me.

It is true that I was the first person ever to capture Gellert Grindelwald and also true that Albus Dumbledore was something more than a schoolteacher to me. More than this I cannot say without fear of breaching the Official Magical Secrets Act or, more importantly, the confidences that Dumbledore, most private of men, placed in me.

Fantastic Beasts and Where to Find Them was a labour of love in more ways than one. As I look back over this early book, I relive memories that are etched on every page, though invisible to the reader. It is my fondest hope that a new generation of witches and wizards will find in its pages fresh reason to love and protect the incredible beasts with whom we share magic.

Newt Scamander

Editor's note: for Muggle edition,
usual guff: 'obvious fiction – all good
fun – nothing to worry about –
hope you enjoy it'.

Introduction

ABOUT THIS BOOK

FANTASTIC BEASTS *and Where to Find Them* represents the fruit of many years' travel and research. I look back across the years to the seven-year-old wizard who spent hours in his bedroom dismembering Horklumps and I envy him the journeys to come: from darkest jungle to brightest desert, from mountain peak to marshy bog, that grubby Horklump-encrusted boy would track, as he grew up, the beasts described in the following pages. I have visited lairs, burrows and nests across five continents, observed the curious habits of magical beasts in a hundred countries, witnessed their powers, gained their trust and, on occasion, beaten them off with my travelling kettle.

The first edition of *Fantastic Beasts* was commissioned back in 1918 by Mr Augustus Worme of Obscurus Books, who was kind enough to ask me whether I would consider writing an authoritative compendium of magical creatures for his publishing house. I was then but a lowly Ministry of Magic employee and leapt at the chance both to augment my pitiful salary of two Sickles a week and to spend my holidays travelling the globe in search of new magical species. The rest is publishing history.

This Introduction is intended to answer a few of the most frequently asked questions that have been arriving in my weekly postbag ever since this book was first published in 1927. The first of these is that most fundamental question of all — what is a 'beast'?

WHAT IS A BEAST?

THE DEFINITION OF a 'beast' has caused controversy for centuries. Though this might surprise some first-time students of Magizoology, the problem might come into clearer focus if we take a moment to consider three types of magical creature.

Werewolves spend most of their time as humans (whether wizard or Muggle). Once a month, however, they transform into savage, four-legged beasts of murderous intent and no human conscience.

The centaurs' habits are not human-like; they live in the wild, refuse clothing, prefer to live apart from wizards and Muggles alike and yet have intelligence equal to theirs.

Trolls bear a humanoid appearance, walk upright, may be taught a few simple words and yet are less intelligent than the dullest unicorn and possess no magical powers in their own right except for their prodigious and unnatural strength.

We now ask ourselves: which of these creatures is a 'being' – that is to say, a creature worthy of legal rights and a voice in the governance of the magical world – and which is a 'beast'?

Early attempts at deciding which magical creatures should be designated 'beasts' were extremely crude.

Burdock Muldoon, Chief of the Wizards' Council[1] in the fourteenth century, decreed that any member of the magical community that walked on two legs would henceforth be granted the status of 'being', all others to remain 'beasts'. In a spirit of friendship he summoned all 'beings' to meet with the wizards at a summit to discuss new magical laws and found to his intense dismay that he had miscalculated. The meeting hall was crammed with goblins who had brought with them as many two-legged creatures as they could find. As Bathilda Bagshot tells us in *A History of Magic*:

> *Little could be heard over the squawking of the Diricawls, the moaning of the Augureys and the relentless, piercing song of the Fwoopers. As wizards and witches attempted to consult the papers before them, sundry pixies and fairies whirled around their heads, giggling and jabbering. A dozen or so trolls began to smash apart the chamber with their clubs, while hags glided about the place in search of children to eat. The Council Chief stood up to open the meeting, slipped on a pile of Porlock dung and ran cursing from the hall.*

As we see, the mere possession of two legs was no guarantee that a magical creature could or would take an interest in the affairs of wizard government. Embittered, Burdock Muldoon forswore any further attempts to integrate non-wizard members of the magical community into the Wizards' Council.

---

1. The Wizards' Council preceded the Ministry of Magic.

Muldoon's successor, Madame Elfrida Clagg, attempted to redefine 'beings' in the hope of creating closer ties with other magical creatures. 'Beings', she declared, were those who could speak the human tongue. All those who could make themselves understood to Council members were therefore invited to join the next meeting. Once again, however, there were problems. Trolls who had been taught a few simple sentences by the goblins proceeded to destroy the hall as before. Jarveys raced around the Council's chair legs, tearing at as many ankles as they could reach. Meanwhile a large delegation of ghosts (who had been barred under Muldoon's leadership on the grounds that they did not walk on two legs, but glided) attended but left in disgust at what they later termed 'the Council's unashamed emphasis on the needs of the living as opposed to the wishes of the dead'. The centaurs, who under Muldoon had been classified as 'beasts' and were now under Madame Clagg defined as 'beings', refused to attend the Council in protest at the exclusion of the merpeople, who were unable to converse in anything except Mermish while above water.

Not until 1811 were definitions found that most of the magical community found acceptable.

Grogan Stump, the newly appointed Minister for Magic, decreed that a 'being' was 'any creature that has sufficient intelligence to understand the laws of the magical community and to bear part of the responsibility in shaping those laws'.[2] Troll representatives were questioned in the absence of goblins and judged not to understand anything that was being said to them; they were therefore classified as 'beasts' despite their two-legged gait; merpeople were invited through translators to become 'beings' for the first time; fairies, pixies and gnomes, despite their humanoid appearance, were placed firmly in the 'beast' category.

Naturally, the matter has not rested there. We are all familiar with the extremists who campaign for the classification of Muggles as 'beasts'; we are all aware that the centaurs have refused 'being' status and requested to remain 'beasts';[3] werewolves, meanwhile, have been shunted between the Beast and Being divisions for many years; at the time of writing there is an office for Werewolf Support Services at the Being Division whereas the Werewolf Registry and Werewolf Capture Unit fall under the Beast Division. Several highly intelligent creatures are classified as 'beasts' because they are incapable of overcoming their own brutal natures. Acromantulas and Manticores are capable of intelligent speech but

---

2. An exception was made for the ghosts, who asserted that it was insensitive to class them as 'beings' when they were so clearly 'has-beens'. Stump therefore created the three divisions of the Department for the Regulation and Control of Magical Creatures that exist today: the Beast Division, the Being Division and the Spirit Division.

3. The centaurs objected to some of the creatures with whom they were asked to share 'being' status, such as hags and vampires, and declared that they would

manage their own affairs separately from wizards. A year later the merpeople made the same request. The Ministry of Magic accepted their demands reluctantly. Although a Centaur Liaison Office exists in the Beast Division of the Department for the Regulation and Control of Magical Creatures, no centaur has ever used it. Indeed, 'being sent to the Centaur Office' has become an in-joke at the Department and means that the person in question is shortly to be fired.

will attempt to devour any human that goes near them. The sphinx talks only in puzzles and riddles, and is violent when given the wrong answer.

Wherever there is continued uncertainty about the classification of a beast in the following pages, I have noted it in the entry for that creature.

Let us now turn to the one question that witches and wizards ask more than any other when the conversation turns to Magizoology: why don't Muggles notice these creatures?

A BRIEF HISTORY OF MUGGLE AWARENESS OF FANTASTIC BEASTS

ASTONISHING THOUGH it may seem to many wizards, Muggles have not always been ignorant of the magical and monstrous creatures that we have worked so long and hard to hide. A glance through Muggle art and literature of the Middle Ages reveals that many of the creatures they now believe to be imaginary were then known to be real. The dragon, the griffin, the unicorn, the phoenix, the centaur — these and more are represented in Muggle works of that period, though usually with almost comical inexactitude.

However, a closer examination of Muggle bestiaries of that period demonstrates that most magical beasts either escaped Muggle notice completely or were mistaken for something else. Examine this surviving fragment of manuscript, written by one Brother Benedict, a Franciscan monk from Worcestershire:

Todaye while travailing in the Herbe Garden, I did push aside the basil to discover a Ferret of monstrous size. It did not run nor hide as Ferrets are wont to do, but leapt upon me, throwing me backwards upon the grounde and crying with most unnatural fury, 'Get out of it, baldy!' It did then bite my nose so viciously that I did bleed for several Hours. The Friar was unwillinge to believe that I had met a talking Ferret and did ask me whether I had been supping of Brother Boniface's Turnip Wine. As my nose was still swollen and bloody I was excused Vespers.

Evidently our Muggle friend had unearthed not a ferret, as he supposed, but a Jarvey, most likely in pursuit of its favourite prey, gnomes.

Imperfect understanding is often more dangerous than ignorance, and the Muggles' fear of magic was undoubtedly increased by their dread of what might be lurking in their herb gardens. Muggle persecution of wizards at this time was reaching a pitch hitherto unknown and sightings of such beasts as dragons and Hippogriffs were contributing to Muggle hysteria.

It is not the aim of this work to discuss the

dark days that preceded the wizards' retreat into hiding.[4] All that concerns us here is the fate of those fabulous beasts that, like ourselves, would have to be concealed if Muggles were ever to be convinced there was no such thing as magic.

The International Confederation of Wizards argued the matter out at their famous summit meeting of 1692. No fewer than seven weeks of sometimes acrimonious discussion between wizards of all nationalities were devoted to the troublesome question of magical creatures. How many species would we be able to conceal from Muggle notice and which should they be? Where and how should we hide them? The debate raged on, some creatures oblivious to the fact that their destiny was being decided, others contributing to the debate.[5]

At last agreement was reached.[6] Twenty-seven species, ranging in size from dragons to Bundimuns, were to be hidden from Muggles so as to create the illusion that they had never existed outside the imagination. This number was increased over the following century, as wizards became more confident in their methods of concealment. In 1750, Clause 73 was inserted in the International Statute of Wizarding Secrecy, to which wizard ministries worldwide conform today:

Each wizarding governing body will be responsible for the concealment, care and control of all magical beasts, beings and spirits dwelling within its territory's borders. Should any such creature cause harm to, or draw the notice of, the Muggle community, that nation's wizarding governing body will be subject to discipline by the International Confederation of Wizards.

4. Anyone interested in a full account of this particularly bloody period of wizarding history should consult *A History of Magic* by Bathilda Bagshot (Little Red Books, 1947).

5. Delegations of centaurs, merpeople and goblins were persuaded to attend the summit.

6. Except by the goblins.

MAGICAL BEASTS IN HIDING

I T WOULD BE IDLE TO deny that there have been occasional breaches of Clause 73 since it was first put in place. Older British readers will remember the Ilfracombe Incident of 1932, when a rogue Welsh Green dragon swooped down upon a crowded beach full of sunbathing Muggles. Fatalities were mercifully prevented by the brave actions of a holidaying wizarding family (subsequently awarded Orders of Merlin, First Class), when they immediately performed the largest batch of Memory Charms this century on the inhabitants of Ilfracombe, thus narrowly averting catastrophe.[7]

The International Confederation of Wizards has had to fine certain nations repeatedly for contravening Clause 73. Tibet and Scotland are two of the most persistent offenders. Muggle sightings of the yeti have been so numerous that the International Confederation of Wizards felt it necessary to station an International Task Force in the mountains on a permanent basis. Meanwhile the world's largest kelpie continues to evade capture in Loch Ness and appears to have developed a positive thirst for publicity.

These unfortunate mishaps notwithstanding, we wizards may congratulate ourselves on a job well done. There can be no doubt that the overwhelming majority of present-day Muggles refuse to believe in the magical beasts their ancestors so feared. Even those Muggles who do notice Porlock droppings or Streeler trails — it would be foolish to suppose that all traces of these creatures can be hidden — appear satisfied with the flimsiest non-magical explanation.[8] If any Muggle is unwise enough to confide in another that he has spotted a Hippogriff winging its way north, he is generally believed to be drunk or a 'loony'. Unfair though this may seem on the Muggle in question, it is nevertheless preferable to being burnt at the stake or drowned in the village duckpond.

So how does the wizarding community hide fantastic beasts?

Luckily, some species do not require much wizarding assistance in avoiding the notice of Muggles. Creatures such as the Tebo, the Demiguise and the Bowtruckle have their own highly effective means of camouflage and no intervention by the Ministry of Magic has ever been necessary on their behalf. Then there are those beasts that, due to cleverness or innate shyness, avoid contact with Muggles at all costs — for instance, the unicorn, the Mooncalf and the centaur. Other magical creatures inhabit places inaccessible to Muggles — one thinks of the Acromantula, deep in the uncharted jungle of Borneo, and the phoenix,

---

7. In his 1972 book *Muggles Who Notice*, Blenheim Stalk asserts that some residents of Ilfracombe escaped the Mass Memory Charm. 'To this day, a Muggle bearing the nickname "Dodgy Dirk" holds forth in bars along the south coast on the subject of a "dirty great flying lizard" that punctured his lilo.'

8. For a fascinating examination of this fortunate tendency of Muggles, the reader might like to consult *The Philosophy of the Mundane: Why the Muggles Prefer Not to Know*, Professor Mordicus Egg (Dust & Mildewe, 1963).

nesting high on mountain peaks unreachable without the use of magic. Finally, and most commonly, we have beasts that are too small, too speedy or too adept at passing for mundane animals to attract a Muggle's attention – Chizpurfles, Billywigs and Crups fall into this category.

Nevertheless there are still plenty of beasts that, whether wilfully or inadvertently, remain conspicuous even to the Muggle eye, and it is these that create a significant amount of work for the Department for the Regulation and Control of Magical Creatures. This department, the second largest at the Ministry of Magic,[9] deals with the varying needs of the many species under its care in a variety of different ways.

SAFE HABITATS

Perhaps the most important step in the concealment of magical creatures is the creation of safe habitats. Muggle-repelling charms prevent trespassers into the forests where centaurs and unicorns live and on the lakes and rivers set aside for the use of merpeople. In extreme cases, such as that of the Quintaped, whole areas have been made unplottable.[10]

Some of these safe areas must be kept under constant wizarding supervision; for example, dragon reservations. While unicorns and merpeople are only too happy to stay within the territories designated for their use, dragons will seek any

opportunity to set forth in search of prey beyond the reservation borders. In some cases Muggle-repelling charms will not work, as the beast's own powers will cancel them. Cases in point are the kelpie, whose sole aim in life is to attract humans towards it, and the Pogrebin, which seeks out humans for itself.

CONTROLS ON SELLING AND BREEDING

The possibility of a Muggle being alarmed by any of the larger or more dangerous magical beasts has been greatly reduced by the severe penalties now attached to their breeding and the sale of their young and eggs. The Department for the Regulation and Control of Magical Creatures keeps a strict watch on the trade in fantastic beasts. The 1965 Ban on Experimental Breeding has made the creation of new species illegal.

DISILLUSIONMENT CHARMS

The wizard on the street also plays a part in the concealment of magical beasts. Those who own a Hippogriff, for example, are bound by law to enchant the beast with a Disillusionment Charm to distort the vision of any Muggle who may see it. Disillusionment Charms should be performed daily, as their effects are apt to wear off.

9. The largest department at the Ministry of Magic is the Department of Magical Law Enforcement, to which the remaining six departments are all, in some respect, answerable – with the possible exception of the Department of Mysteries.

10. When an area of land is made unplottable, it is impossible to chart on maps.

MEMORY CHARMS

When the worst happens and a Muggle sees what he or she is not supposed to see, the Memory Charm is perhaps the most useful repair tool. The Memory Charm may be performed by the owner of the beast in question, but in severe cases of Muggle notice, a team of trained Obliviators may be sent in by the Ministry of Magic.

THE OFFICE OF MISINFORMATION

The Office of Misinformation will become involved in only the very worst magical–Muggle collisions. Some magical catastrophes or accidents are simply too glaringly obvious to be explained away by Muggles without the help of an outside authority. The Office of Misinformation will in such a case liaise directly with the Muggle prime minister to seek a plausible non-magical explanation for the event. The unstinting efforts of this office in persuading Muggles that all photographic evidence of the Loch Ness kelpie is fake have gone some way to salvaging a situation that at one time looked exceedingly dangerous.

WHY MAGIZOOLOGY MATTERS

THE MEASURES described above merely hint at the full scope and extent of the work done by the Department for the Regulation and Control of Magical Creatures. It remains only to answer that question to which we all, in our hearts, know the answer: why do we continue, as a community and as individuals, to attempt to protect and conceal magical beasts, even those that are savage and untameable? The answer is, of course: to ensure that future generations of witches and wizards enjoy their strange beauty and powers as we have been privileged to do.

I offer this work as a mere introduction to the wealth of fantastic beasts that inhabit our world. Eighty-one species are described in the following pages, but I do not doubt that more will be discovered, necessitating another revised edition of *Fantastic Beasts and Where to Find Them*. In the meantime I will merely add that it affords me great pleasure to think that generations of young witches and wizards have grown to a fuller knowledge and understanding of the fantastic beasts I love through the pages of this book.

MINISTRY OF MAGIC CLASSIFICATIONS

THE DEPARTMENT for the Regulation and Control of Magical Creatures gives classifications to all known beasts, beings and spirits. These offer an at-a-glance guide to the perceived dangerousness of a creature. The five categories are as follows:

Ministry of Magic (M.O.M.) Classification

XXXXX	Known wizard killer/impossible to train or domesticate
XXXX	Dangerous/requires specialist knowledge/skilled wizard may handle
XXX	Competent wizard should cope
XX	Harmless/may be domesticated
X	Boring

CHINESE FIREBALL
(sometimes known as LIONDRAGON)

M.O.M. Classification: XXXXX

In some cases I have felt an explanation for the classification of a particular beast is necessary and have added footnotes accordingly.

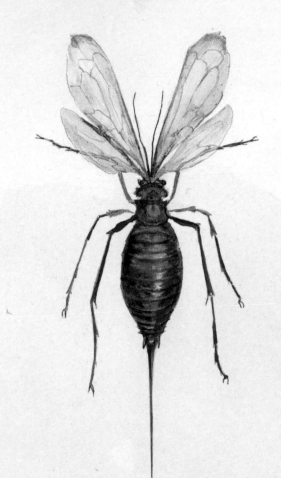

an A–Z of
FANTASTIC
BEASTS

2

Acromantula eggs are defined as Class A Non-Tradeable Goods

ACROMANTULA

M.O.M. Classification: XXXXX

THE ACROMANTULA is a monstrous eight-eyed spider capable of human speech. It originated in Borneo, where it inhabits dense jungle. Its distinctive features include the thick black hair that covers its body; its legspan, which may reach up to fifteen feet; its pincers, which produce a distinctive clicking sound when the Acromantula is excited or angry; and a poisonous secretion. The Acromantula is carnivorous and prefers large prey. It spins dome-shaped webs upon the ground. The female is bigger than the male and may lay up to one hundred eggs at a time. Soft and white, these are as large as beach balls. The young hatch in six to eight weeks. Acromantula eggs are defined as Class A Non-Tradeable Goods by the Department for the Regulation and Control of Magical Creatures, meaning that severe penalties are attached to their importation or sale.

This beast is believed to be wizard-bred, possibly intended to guard wizard dwellings or treasure, as is often the case with magically created monsters.[1] Despite its near-human intelligence, the Acromantula is untrainable and highly dangerous to wizard and Muggle alike.

Rumours that a colony of Acromantula has been established in Scotland are unconfirmed.

1. Beasts capable of human speech are rarely self-taught; an exception is the Jarvey. The Ban on Experimental Breeding did not come into effect until this century, long after the first recorded sighting of an Acromantula in 1794.

ASHWINDER

M.O.M. Classification: XXX

THE ASHWINDER is created when a magical fire[2] is allowed to burn unchecked for too long. A thin, pale-grey serpent with glowing red eyes, it will rise from the embers of an unsupervised fire and slither away into the shadows of the dwelling in which it finds itself, leaving an ashy trail behind it.

The Ashwinder lives for only an hour and during that time seeks a dark and secluded spot in which to lay its eggs, after which it will collapse into dust. Ashwinder eggs are brilliant red and give off intense heat. They will ignite the dwelling within minutes if not found and frozen with a suitable charm. Any wizard realising that one or more Ashwinders are loose in the house must trace them immediately and locate the nest of eggs. Once frozen, these eggs are of great value for use in Love Potions and may be eaten whole as a cure for ague.

Ashwinders are found worldwide.

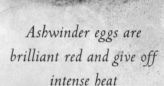

Ashwinder eggs are brilliant red and give off intense heat

AUGUREY

(also known as IRISH PHOENIX)

M.O.M. Classification: XX

THE AUGUREY is a native of Britain and Ireland, though sometimes found elsewhere in northern Europe. A thin and mournful-looking bird, somewhat like a small and underfed vulture in appearance, the Augurey is greenish black. It is intensely shy, nests in bramble and thorn, eats large insects and fairies, flies only in heavy rain and otherwise remains hidden in its tear-shaped nest.

The Augurey has a distinctive low and throbbing cry, which was once believed to foretell death. Wizards avoided Augurey nests for fear of hearing that heart-rending sound, and more than one wizard is believed to have suffered a heart attack on passing a thicket and hearing an unseen Augurey wail.[3] Patient research eventually revealed, however, that the Augurey merely sings at the approach of rain.[4] The Augurey has since enjoyed a vogue as a home weather forecaster, though many find its almost continual moaning during the winter months difficult to bear. Augurey feathers are useless as quills because they repel ink.

2. Any fire to which a magical substance such as Floo powder has been added.
3. Uric the Oddball is known to have slept in a room containing no fewer than fifty pet Augureys. During one particularly wet winter, Uric became convinced by the moaning of his Augureys that he had died and was now a ghost. His subsequent attempts to walk through the walls of his house resulted in what his biographer Radolphus Pittiman describes as a 'concussion of ten days' duration'.
4. See *Why I Didn't Die When the Augurey Cried* by Gulliver Pokeby (Little Red Books, 1824).

BASILISK

M.O.M. Classification: XXXXX

THE FIRST RECORDED Basilisk was bred by Herpo the Foul, a Greek Dark wizard and Parselmouth, who discovered after much experimentation that a chicken egg hatched beneath a toad would produce a gigantic serpent possessed of extraordinarily dangerous powers.

The Basilisk is a brilliant green serpent that may reach up to fifty feet in length. The male has a scarlet plume upon its head. It has exceptionally venomous fangs but its most dangerous means of attack is the gaze of its large yellow eyes. Anyone looking directly into these will suffer instant death.

If the food source is sufficient (the Basilisk will eat all mammals and birds and most reptiles), the serpent may attain a very great age. Herpo the Foul's Basilisk is believed to have lived for close on nine hundred years.

The creation of Basilisks has been illegal since medieval times, although the practice is easily concealed by simply removing the chicken egg from beneath the toad when the Department for the Regulation and Control of Magical Creatures comes to call. However, since Basilisks are uncontrollable except by Parselmouths, they are as dangerous to most Dark wizards as to anybody else, and there have been no recorded sightings of Basilisks in Britain for at least four hundred years.

A chicken egg hatched beneath a toad would produce a gigantic serpent possessed of extraordinarily dangerous powers

BILLYWIG

M.O.M. Classification: XXX

1. Billywig
found at Kata Tjuta, November

T HE BILLYWIG is an insect native to Australia. It is around half an inch long and a vivid sapphire blue, although its speed is such that it is rarely noticed by Muggles and often not by wizards until they have been stung. The Billywig's wings are attached to the top of its head and are rotated very fast so that it spins as it flies. At the bottom of the body is a long thin sting. Those who have been stung by a Billywig suffer giddiness followed by levitation. Generations of young Australian witches and wizards have attempted to catch Billywigs and provoke them into stinging in order to enjoy these side effects, though too many stings may cause the victim to hover uncontrollably for days on end, and where there is a severe allergic reaction, permanent floating may ensue. Dried Billywig stings are used in several potions and are believed to be a component in the popular sweet Fizzing Whizzbees.

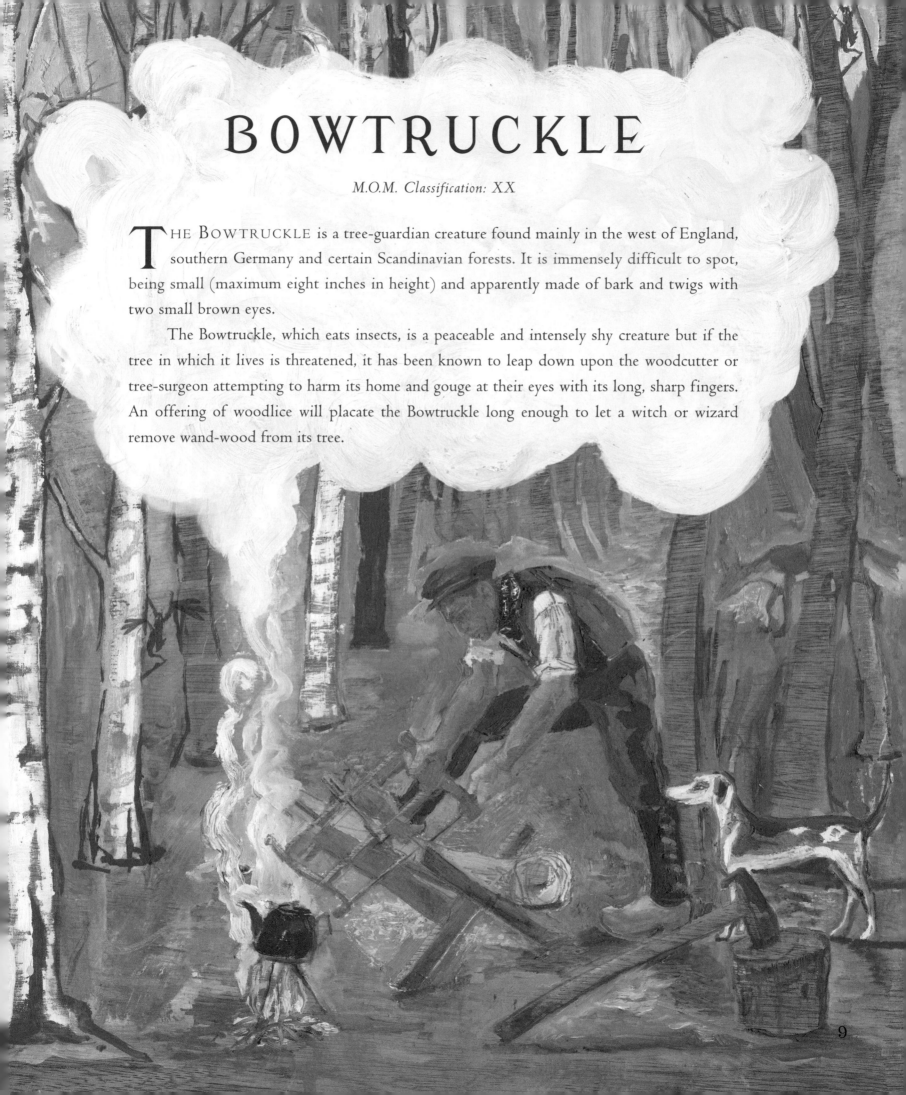

BOWTRUCKLE

M.O.M. Classification: XX

THE BOWTRUCKLE is a tree-guardian creature found mainly in the west of England, southern Germany and certain Scandinavian forests. It is immensely difficult to spot, being small (maximum eight inches in height) and apparently made of bark and twigs with two small brown eyes.

The Bowtruckle, which eats insects, is a peaceable and intensely shy creature but if the tree in which it lives is threatened, it has been known to leap down upon the woodcutter or tree-surgeon attempting to harm its home and gouge at their eyes with its long, sharp fingers. An offering of woodlice will placate the Bowtruckle long enough to let a witch or wizard remove wand-wood from its tree.

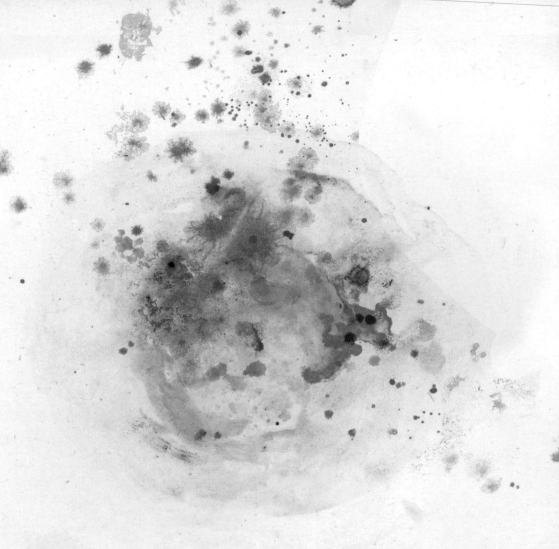

BUNDIMUN

M.O.M. Classification: XXX

BUNDIMUNS ARE found worldwide. Skilled at creeping under floorboards and behind skirting boards, they infest houses. The presence of a Bundimun is usually announced by a foul stench of decay. The Bundimun oozes a secretion which rots away the very foundations of the dwelling in which it is found.

The Bundimun at rest resembles a patch of greenish fungus with eyes, though when alarmed it will scuttle away on its numerous spindly legs. It feeds on dirt. Scouring charms will rid a house of an infestation of Bundimuns, though if they have been allowed to grow too large, the Department for the Regulation and Control of Magical Creatures (Pest Sub-Division) should be contacted before the house collapses. Diluted Bundimun secretion is used in certain magical cleaning fluids.

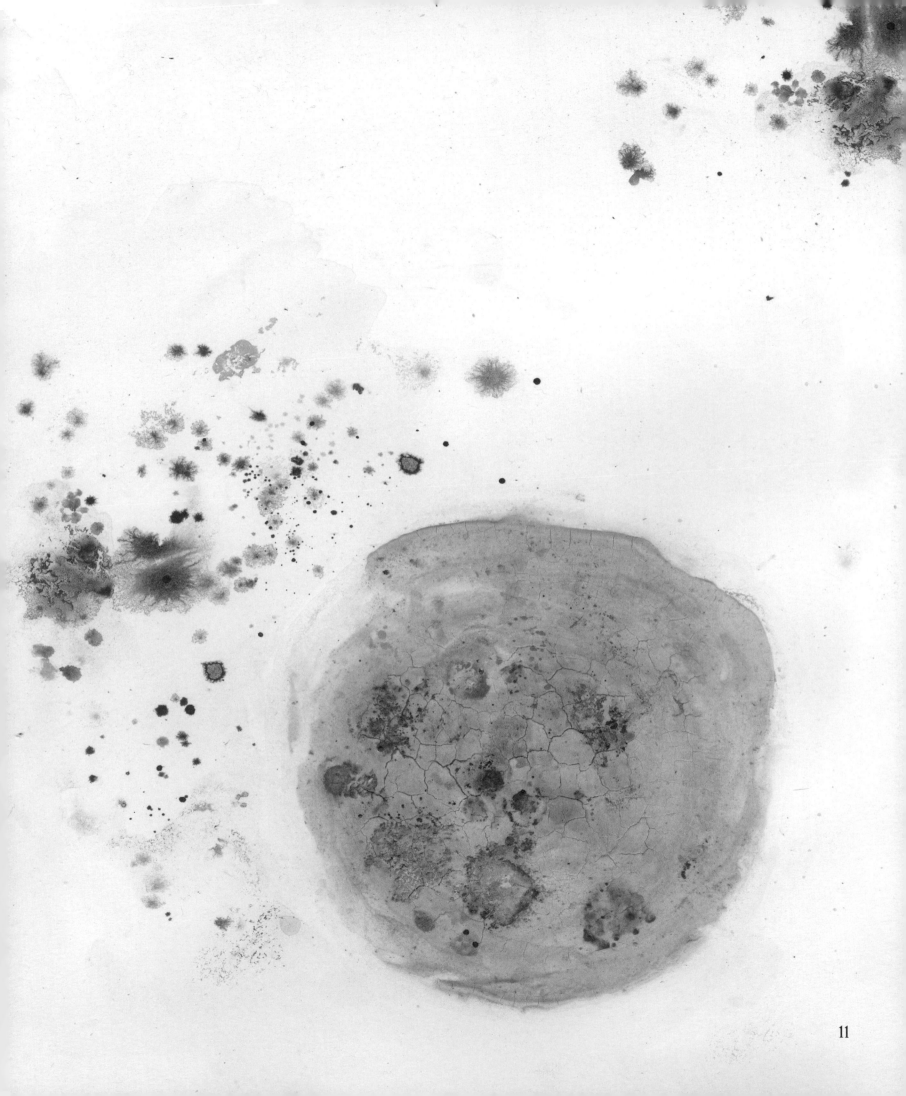

11

CENTAUR

M.O.M. Classification: XXXX[5]

THE CENTAUR has a human head, torso and arms joined to a horse's body which may be any of several colours. Being intelligent and capable of speech, it should not strictly speaking be termed a beast, but by its own request it has been classified as such by the Ministry of Magic (see the Introduction to this book).

The centaur is forest-dwelling. Centaurs are believed to have originated in Greece, though there are now centaur communities in many parts of Europe. Wizarding authorities in each of the countries where centaurs are found have allocated areas where the centaurs will not be troubled by Muggles; however, centaurs stand in little need of wizard protection, having their own means of hiding from humans.

The ways of the centaur are shrouded in mystery. They are generally speaking as mistrustful of wizards as they are of Muggles and indeed seem to make little differentiation between us. They live in herds ranging in size from ten to fifty members. They are reputed to be well versed in magical healing, divination, archery and astronomy.

5. The centaur is given an XXXX classification not because it is unduly aggressive, but because it should be treated with great respect. The same applies to merpeople and unicorns.

CHIMAERA

M.O.M. Classification: XXXXX

THE CHIMAERA is a rare Greek monster with a lion's head, a goat's body and a dragon's tail. Vicious and bloodthirsty, the Chimaera is extremely dangerous. There is only one known instance of the successful slaying of a Chimaera and the unlucky wizard concerned fell to his death from his winged horse (see below) shortly afterwards, exhausted by his efforts. Chimaera eggs are classified as Grade A Non-Tradeable Goods.

*Vicious and bloodthirsty,
the Chimaera is
extremely dangerous*

15

CHIZPURFLE

M.O.M. Classification: XX

CHIZPURFLES ARE small parasites up to a twentieth of an inch high, crab-like in appearance with large fangs. They are attracted by magic and may infest the fur and feathers of such creatures as Crups and Augureys. They will also enter wizard dwellings and attack magical objects such as wands, gradually gnawing their way through to the magical core, or else settle in dirty cauldrons, where they will gorge upon any lingering drops of potion.[6] Though Chizpurfles are easy enough to destroy with any of a number of patented potions on the market, severe infestations may require a visit from the Pest Sub-Division of the Department for the Regulation and Control of Magical Creatures, as Chizpurfles swollen with magical substances will prove very hard to fight.

6. In the absence of magic, Chizpurfles have been known to attack electrical objects from within (for a fuller understanding of what electricity is, see *Home Life and Social Habits of British Muggles,* Wilhelm Wigworthy, Little Red Books, 1987). Chizpurfle infestations explain the puzzling failure of many relatively new Muggle electrical artefacts.

Crab-like in appearance with large fangs

CLABBERT

M.O.M. Classification: XX

THE CLABBERT is a tree-dwelling creature, in appearance something like a cross between a monkey and a frog. It originated in the southern states of America, though it has since been exported worldwide. The smooth and hairless skin is a mottled green, the hands and feet are webbed, and the arms and legs are long and supple, enabling the Clabbert to swing between branches with the agility of an orang-utan. The head has short horns and the wide mouth, which appears to be grinning, is full of razor-sharp teeth. The Clabbert feeds mostly on small lizards and birds.

The Clabbert's most distinctive feature is the large pustule in the middle of its forehead, which turns scarlet and flashes when it senses danger. American wizards once kept Clabberts in their gardens to give early warning of approaching Muggles, but the International Confederation of Wizards has introduced fines which have largely ended this practice. The sight of a tree at night full of glowing Clabbert pustules, while decorative, attracted too many Muggles wishing to ask why their neighbours still had their Christmas lights up in June.

The Clabbert's most distinctive feature is the large pustule in the middle of its forehead

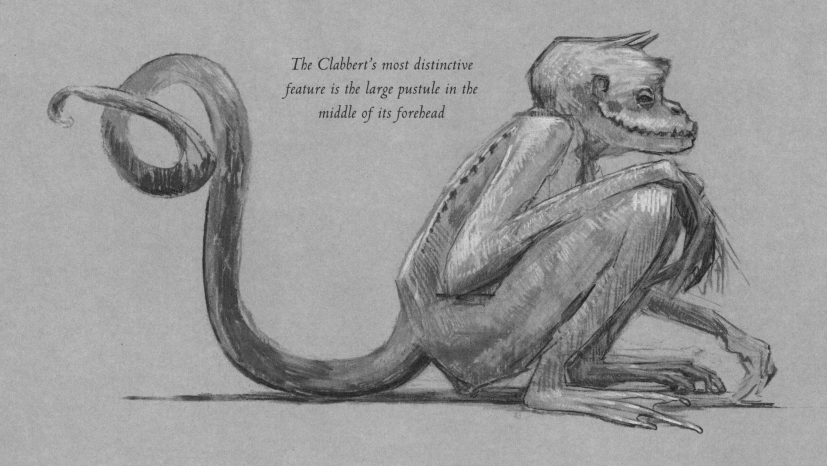

18

CRUP

M.O.M. Classification: XXX

THE CRUP originated in the southeast of England. It closely resembles a Jack Russell terrier, except for the forked tail. The Crup is almost certainly a wizard-created dog, as it is intensely loyal to wizards and ferocious towards Muggles. It is a great scavenger, eating anything from gnomes to old tyres. Crup licences may be obtained from the Department for the Regulation and Control of Magical Creatures on completion of a simple test to prove that the applicant wizard is capable of controlling the Crup in Muggle-inhabited areas. Crup owners are legally obliged to remove the Crup's tail with a painless Severing Charm while the Crup is six to eight weeks old, lest Muggles notice it.

It closely resembles a Jack Russell terrier, except for the forked tail

DEMIGUISE

M.O.M. Classification: XXXX

T HE DEMIGUISE is found in the Far East, though only with great difficulty, for this beast is able to make itself invisible when threatened and can be seen only by wizards skilled in its capture. The Demiguise is a peaceful herbivorous beast, something like a graceful ape in appearance, with large, black, doleful eyes more often than not hidden by its hair. The whole body is covered with long, fine, silky, silvery hair. Demiguise pelts are highly valued as the hair may be spun into Invisibility Cloaks.

DIRICAWL

M.O.M. Classification: XX

THE DIRICAWL originated in Mauritius. A plump-bodied, fluffy-feathered, flightless bird, the Diricawl is remarkable for its method of escaping danger. It can vanish in a puff of feathers and reappear elsewhere (the phoenix shares this ability; see below).

Interestingly, Muggles were once fully aware of the existence of the Diricawl, though they knew it by the name of 'dodo'. Unaware that the Diricawl could vanish at will, Muggles believe they have hunted the species to extinction. As this seems to have raised Muggle awareness of the dangers of slaying their fellow creatures indiscriminately, the International Confederation of Wizards has never deemed it appropriate that the Muggles should be made aware of the continued existence of the Diricawl.

A plump-bodied, fluffy-feathered, flightless bird

DOXY

(sometimes known as BITING FAIRY)

M.O.M. Classification: XXX

THE DOXY IS OFTEN mistaken for a fairy (see below) though it is a quite separate species. Like the fairy, it has a minute human form, though in the Doxy's case this is covered in thick black hair and has an extra pair of arms and legs. The Doxy's wings are thick, curved and shiny, much like a beetle's. Doxys are found throughout northern Europe and America, preferring cold climates. They lay up to five hundred eggs at a time and bury them. The eggs hatch in two to three weeks.

Doxys have double rows of sharp, venomous teeth. An antidote should be taken if bitten.

DRAGON

M.O.M. Classification: XXXXX

PROBABLY THE MOST famous of all magical beasts, dragons are among the most difficult to hide. The female is generally larger and more aggressive than the male, though neither should be approached by any but highly skilled and trained wizards. Dragon hide, blood, heart, liver and horn all have highly magical properties, but dragon eggs are defined as Class A Non-Tradeable Goods.

There are ten breeds of dragon, though these have been known to interbreed on occasion, producing rare hybrids. Pure-bred dragons are as follows:

ANTIPODEAN
OPALEYE

THE OPALEYE is a native of New Zealand, though it has been known to migrate to Australia when territory becomes scarce in its native land. Unusually for a dragon, it dwells in valleys rather than mountains. It is of medium size (between two and three tonnes). Perhaps the most beautiful type of dragon, it has iridescent, pearly scales and glittering, multi-coloured, pupil-less eyes, hence its name. This dragon produces a very vivid scarlet flame, though by dragon standards it is not particularly aggressive and will rarely kill unless hungry. Its favourite food is sheep, though it has been known to attack larger prey. A spate of kangaroo killings in the late 1970s were attributed to a male Opaleye ousted from his homeland by a dominant female. Opaleye eggs are pale grey and may be mistaken for fossils by unwary Muggles.

CHINESE FIREBALL

(sometimes known as LIONDRAGON)

THE ONLY ORIENTAL dragon has a particularly striking appearance. Scarlet and smooth-scaled, it has a fringe of golden spikes around its snub-snouted face and extremely protuberant eyes. The Fireball gained its name for the mushroom-shaped flame that bursts from its nostrils when it is angered. It weighs between two and four tonnes, the female being larger than the male. Eggs are a vivid crimson speckled with gold and the shells are much prized for use in Chinese wizardry. The Fireball is aggressive but more tolerant of its own species than most dragons, sometimes consenting to share its territory with up to two others. The Fireball will feast on most mammals, though it prefers pigs and humans.

The Fireball gained its name for the mushroom-shaped flame that bursts from its nostrils when it is angered

28

COMMON WELSH GREEN

THE WELSH GREEN blends well with the lush grass of its homeland, though it nests in the higher mountains, where a reservation has been established for its preservation. The Ilfracombe Incident notwithstanding (see Introduction), this breed is among the least troublesome of the dragons, preferring, like the Opaleye, to prey on sheep and actively avoiding humans unless provoked. The Welsh Green has an easily recognisable and surprisingly melodious roar. Fire is issued in thin jets. The Welsh Green's eggs are an earthy brown, flecked with green.

HEBRIDEAN BLACK

RITAIN'S OTHER native dragon is more aggressive than its Welsh counterpart. It requires a territory of as much as a hundred square miles per dragon. Up to thirty feet in length, the Hebridean Black is rough-scaled, with brilliant purple eyes and a line of shallow but razor-sharp ridges along its back. Its tail is tipped by an arrow-shaped spike and it has bat-like wings. The Hebridean Black feeds mostly on deer, though it has been known to carry off large dogs and even cattle. The wizard clan MacFusty, who have dwelled in the Hebrides for centuries, have traditionally taken responsibility for the management of their native dragons.

HUNGARIAN HORNTAIL

The Hungarian Horntail feeds on goats, sheep and, whenever possible, humans

SUPPOSEDLY THE MOST dangerous of all dragon breeds, the Hungarian Horntail has black scales and is lizard-like in appearance. It has yellow eyes, bronze horns and similarly coloured spikes that protrude from its long tail. The Horntail has one of the longest fire-breathing ranges (up to fifty feet). Its eggs are cement-coloured and particularly hard-shelled; the young club their way out using their tails, whose spikes are well developed at birth. The Hungarian Horntail feeds on goats, sheep and, whenever possible, humans.

NORWEGIAN RIDGEBACK

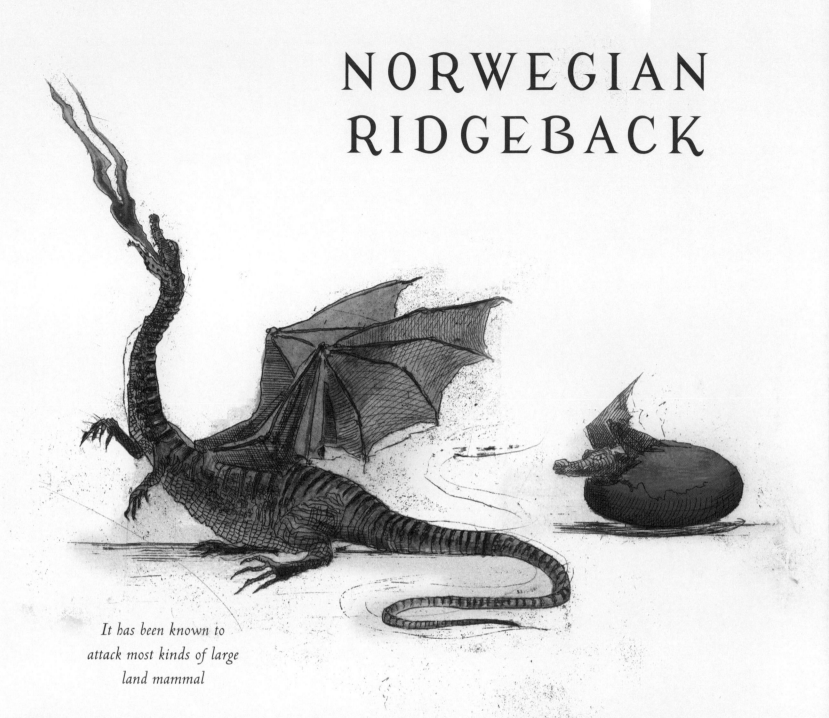

It has been known to attack most kinds of large land mammal

THE NORWEGIAN RIDGEBACK resembles the Horntail in most respects, though instead of tail spikes it sports particularly prominent jet-black ridges along its back. Exceptionally aggressive to its own kind, the Ridgeback is nowadays one of the rarer dragon breeds. It has been known to attack most kinds of large land mammal and, unusually for a dragon, the Ridgeback will also feed on water-dwelling creatures. An unsubstantiated report alleges that a Ridgeback carried off a whale calf off the coast of Norway in 1802. Ridgeback eggs are black and the young develop fire-breathing abilities earlier than other breeds (at between one and three months).

PERUVIAN VIPERTOOTH

THIS IS THE SMALLEST of all known dragons, and the swiftest in flight. A mere fifteen feet or so in length, the Peruvian Vipertooth is smooth-scaled and copper-coloured with black ridge markings. The horns are short and the fangs are particularly venomous. The Vipertooth will feed readily on goats and cows, but has such a liking for humans that the International Confederation of Wizards was forced to send in exterminators in the late nineteenth century to reduce Vipertooth numbers, which had been increasing with alarming rapidity.

ROMANIAN LONGHORN

T HE LONGHORN has dark-green scales and long, glittering golden horns with which it gores its prey before roasting it. When powdered, these horns are highly valued as potion ingredients. The native territory of the Longhorn has now become the world's most important dragon reservation, where wizards of all nationalities study a variety of dragons at close range. The Longhorn has been the subject of an intensive breeding programme because its numbers have fallen so low in recent years, largely because of the trade in its horns, which are now defined as a Class B Tradeable Material.

SWEDISH SHORT-SNOUT

THE SWEDISH SHORT-SNOUT is an attractive silvery-blue dragon whose skin is sought after for the manufacture of protective gloves and shields. The flame that issues from its nostrils is a brilliant blue and can reduce timber and bone to ash in a matter of seconds. The Short-Snout has fewer human killings to its name than most dragons, though as it prefers to live in wild and uninhabited mountainous areas, this is not much to its credit.

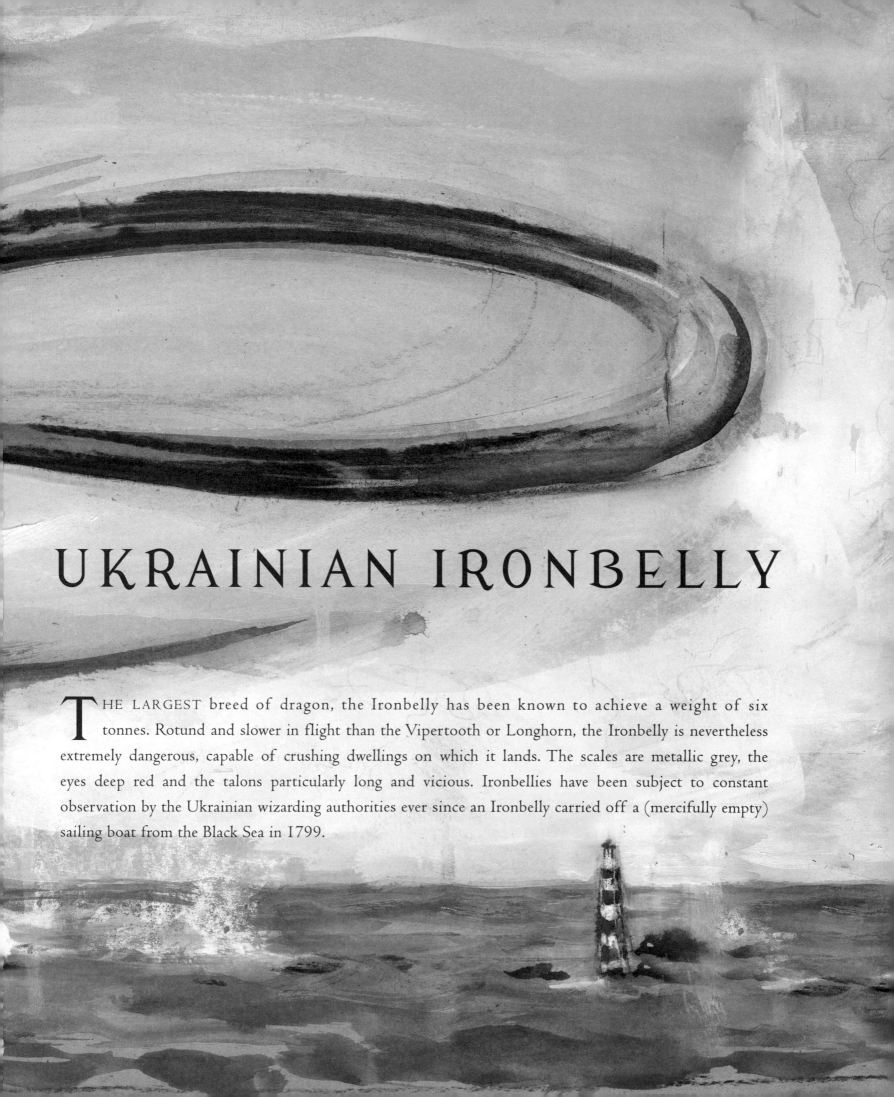

UKRAINIAN IRONBELLY

THE LARGEST breed of dragon, the Ironbelly has been known to achieve a weight of six tonnes. Rotund and slower in flight than the Vipertooth or Longhorn, the Ironbelly is nevertheless extremely dangerous, capable of crushing dwellings on which it lands. The scales are metallic grey, the eyes deep red and the talons particularly long and vicious. Ironbellies have been subject to constant observation by the Ukrainian wizarding authorities ever since an Ironbelly carried off a (mercifully empty) sailing boat from the Black Sea in 1799.

DUGBOG

M.O.M. Classification: XXX

THE DUGBOG IS a marsh-dwelling creature found in Europe and North and South America. It resembles a piece of dead wood while stationary, though closer examination will reveal finned paws and very sharp teeth. It glides and slithers through marshland, feeding mainly on small mammals, and will do severe injury to the ankles of human walkers. The Dugbog's favourite food, however, is Mandrake. Mandrake-growers have been known to seize the leaves of one of their prize plants only to find a bloody mangled mess below owing to the attentions of a Dugbog.

An elfish creature which originated in the Black Forest

ERKLING

M.O.M. Classification: XXXX

THE ERKLING is an elfish creature which originated in the Black Forest in Germany. It is larger than a gnome (three feet high on average), with a pointed face and a high-pitched cackle that is particularly entrancing to children, whom it will attempt to lure away from their guardians and eat. Strict controls by the German Ministry of Magic, however, have reduced Erkling killings dramatically over the last few centuries and the last known Erkling attack, upon the six-year-old wizard Bruno Schmidt, resulted in the death of the Erkling when Master Schmidt hit it very hard over the head with his father's collapsible cauldron.

42

ERUMPENT

M.O.M. Classification: XXXX

THE ERUMPENT is a large grey African beast of great power. Weighing up to a tonne, the Erumpent may be mistaken for a rhinoceros at a distance. It has a thick hide that repels most charms and curses, a large, sharp horn upon its nose and a long, rope-like tail. Erumpents give birth to only one calf at a time.

The Erumpent will not attack unless sorely provoked, but should it charge, the results are usually catastrophic. The Erumpent's horn can pierce everything from skin to metal, and contains a deadly fluid which will cause whatever is injected with it to explode.

Erumpent numbers are not great, as males frequently explode each other during the mating season. They are treated with great caution by African wizards. Erumpent horns, tails and the Exploding Fluid are all used in potions, though classified as Class B Tradeable Materials (Dangerous and Subject to Strict Control).

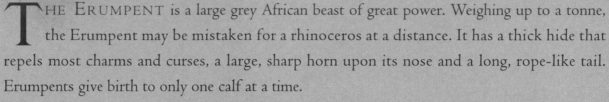

*Weighing up to a tonne,
the Erumpent may be mistaken
for a rhinoceros at a distance*

FAIRY

M.O.M. Classification: XX

THE FAIRY IS a small and decorative beast of little intelligence.[7] Often used or conjured by wizards for decoration, the fairy generally inhabits woodlands or glades. Ranging in height from one to five inches, the fairy has a minute humanoid body, head and limbs but sports large insect-like wings, which may be transparent or multi-coloured, according to type.

The fairy possesses a weak brand of magic that it may use to deter predators, such as the Augurey. It has a quarrelsome nature but, being excessively vain, it will become docile on any occasion when it is called to act as an ornament. Despite its human-like appearance, the fairy cannot speak. It makes a high-pitched buzzing noise to communicate with its fellows.

The fairy lays up to fifty eggs at a time on the underside of leaves. The eggs hatch into brightly coloured larvae. At the age of six to ten days these spin themselves a cocoon, from which they emerge one month later as fully formed winged adults.

FIRE CRAB

M.O.M. Classification: XXX

DESPITE ITS NAME, the Fire Crab greatly resembles a large tortoise with a heavily jewelled shell. In its native Fiji, a stretch of coast has been turned into a reservation for its protection, not only against Muggles, who might be tempted by its valuable shell, but also against unscrupulous wizards, who use the shells as highly prized cauldrons. The Fire Crab does, however, have its own defence mechanism: it shoots flames from its rear end when attacked. Fire Crabs are exported as pets but a special licence is necessary.

---

7. Muggles have a great weakness for fairies, which feature in a variety of tales written for their children. These 'fairy tales' involve winged beings with distinct personalities and the ability to converse as humans (though often in a nauseatingly sentimental fashion). Fairies, as envisaged by the Muggle, inhabit tiny dwellings fashioned out of flower petals, hollowed-out toadstools and similar. They are often depicted as carrying wands. Of all magical beasts the fairy might be said to have received the best Muggle press.

FLOBBERWORM

M.O.M. Classification: X

THE FLOBBERWORM lives in damp ditches. A thick brown worm reaching up to ten inches in length, the Flobberworm moves very little. One end is indistinguishable from the other, both producing the mucus from which its name is derived and which is sometimes used to thicken potions. The Flobberworm's preferred food is lettuce, though it will eat almost any vegetation.

FWOOPER

M.O.M. Classification: XXX

THE FWOOPER is an African bird with extremely vivid plumage; Fwoopers may be orange, pink, lime green or yellow. The Fwooper has long been a provider of fancy quills and also lays brilliantly patterned eggs. Though at first enjoyable, Fwooper song will eventually drive the listener to insanity[8] and the Fwooper is consequently sold with a Silencing Charm upon it, which will need monthly reinforcement. Fwooper owners require licences, as the creatures must be handled responsibly.

8. Uric the Oddball attempted at one time to prove that Fwooper song was actually beneficial to the health and listened to it for three months on end without a break. Unfortunately the Wizards' Council to which he reported his findings were unconvinced, as he had arrived at the meeting wearing nothing but a toupee that on closer inspection proved to be a dead badger.

GHOUL

M.O.M. Classification: XX

THE GHOUL, though ugly, is not a particularly dangerous creature. It resembles a somewhat slimy, buck-toothed ogre and generally resides in attics or barns belonging to wizards, where it eats spiders and moths. It moans and occasionally throws objects around, but is essentially simple-minded and will, at worst, growl alarmingly at anyone who stumbles across it. A Ghoul Task Force exists at the Department for the Regulation and Control of Magical Creatures to remove ghouls from dwellings that have passed into Muggle hands, but in wizarding families the ghoul often becomes a talking point or even a family pet.

GLUMBUMBLE

M.O.M. Classification: XXX

THE GLUMBUMBLE (northern Europe) is a grey, furry-bodied flying insect that produces melancholy-inducing treacle, which is used as an antidote to the hysteria produced by eating Alihotsy leaves. It has been known to infest beehives, with disastrous effects on the honey. Glumbumbles nest in dark and secluded places such as hollow trees and caves. They feed on nettles.

GNOME

M.O.M. Classification: XX

THE GNOME IS a common garden pest found throughout northern Europe and North America. It may reach a foot in height, with a disproportionately large head and hard, bony feet. The gnome can be expelled from the garden by swinging it in circles until dizzy and then dropping it over the garden wall. Alternatively a Jarvey may be used, though many wizards nowadays find this method of gnome-control too brutal.

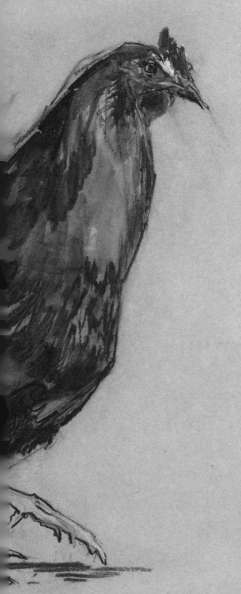

GRAPHORN

M.O.M. Classification: XXXX

THE GRAPHORN is found in mountainous European regions. Large and greyish purple with a humped back, the Graphorn has two very long, sharp horns, walks on large, four-thumbed feet, and has an extremely aggressive nature. Mountain trolls can occasionally be seen mounted on Graphorns, though the latter do not seem to take kindly to attempts to tame them and it is more common to see a troll covered in Graphorn scars. Powdered Graphorn horn is used in many potions, though it is immensely expensive owing to the difficulty in collecting it. Graphorn hide is even tougher than a dragon's and repels most spells.

Griffins are often employed by
wizards to guard treasure

GRIFFIN

M.O.M. Classification: XXXX

THE GRIFFIN originated in Greece and has the front legs and head of a giant eagle, but the body and hind legs of a lion. Like sphinxes (see below), griffins are often employed by wizards to guard treasure. Though griffins are fierce, a handful of skilled wizards have been known to befriend one. Griffins feed on raw meat.

GRINDYLOW

M.O.M. Classification: XX

A HORNED, PALE-GREEN water demon, the Grindylow is found in lakes throughout Britain and Ireland. It feeds on small fish and is aggressive towards wizards and Muggles alike, though merpeople have been known to domesticate it. The Grindylow has very long fingers, which, though they exert a powerful grip, are easy to break.

HIDEBEHIND

M.O.M. Classification: XXXX

THE HIDEBEHIND is an accidentally created species, which was imported to North America by Old World crook Phineas Fletcher. Fletcher, a trader in banned artefacts and creatures, had intended to import a trafficked Demiguise into the New World, with the aim of manufacturing Invisibility Cloaks. The Demiguise escaped on board ship and bred with a stowaway ghoul. Their resultant offspring escaped into Massachusetts' forests when Phineas's ship docked, and their descendants continue to infest the region today. The Hidebehind is nocturnal and has the power of invisibility. Those who have seen it describe a tall, silver-haired creature, something like a skinny bear. Its preferred prey is humans, which Magizoologists speculate is the result of the cruelty with which Phineas Fletcher was known to treat the unfortunate creatures in his power.

57

HIPPOCAMPUS

M.O.M. Classification: XXX

ORIGINATING IN GREECE, the Hippocampus has the head and forequarters of a horse and the tail and hindquarters of a giant fish. Though the species is usually to be found in the Mediterranean, a superb blue roan specimen was caught by merpeople off the shores of Scotland in 1949 and subsequently domesticated by them. The Hippocampus lays large, semi-transparent eggs through which the Tadfoal may be seen.

Large, semi-transparent eggs through which the
Tadfoal may be seen

59

HIPPOGRIFF

M.O.M. Classification: XXX

THE HIPPOGRIFF is native to Europe, though now found worldwide. It has the head of a giant eagle and the body of a horse. It can be tamed, though this should be attempted only by experts. Eye contact should be maintained when approaching a Hippogriff. Bowing shows good intentions. If the Hippogriff returns the greeting, it is safe to draw closer.

The Hippogriff burrows for insects but will also eat birds and small mammals. Breeding Hippogriffs build nests upon the ground into which they will lay a single large and fragile egg, which hatches within twenty-four hours. The fledgling Hippogriff should be ready to fly within a week, though it will be a matter of months before it is able to accompany its parent on longer journeys.

Will lay a single large and fragile egg, which hatches within twenty-four hours

61

HODAG

M.O.M. Classification: XXX

THE HODAG is horned, with red, glowing eyes and long fangs, and the size of a large dog. The Hodag's magic resides largely in its horns which, when powdered, make a man immune to the effects of alcohol and able to go without sleep for seven days and seven nights. Like the Snallygaster, the Hodag is a North American creature whose antics have excited considerable Muggle interest and curiosity. It feeds largely on Mooncalves and is consequently attracted to Muggle farms at night. MACUSA's Department of No-Maj Misinformation has put in considerable work to successfully convince Muggles that sightings of Hodags have been hoaxes. It is now confined, mostly successfully, to a protected area around Wisconsin.

HORKLUMP SPECIMENS

Collected: Scandinavia

Shown in various forms found abundant
across Scandinavia & N. Europe

Predator: Gnomes   Classification: X

HORKLUMP

M.O.M. Classification: X

THE HORKLUMP comes from Scandinavia but is now widespread throughout northern Europe. It resembles a fleshy, pinkish mushroom covered in sparse, wiry black bristles. A prodigious breeder, the Horklump will cover an average garden in a matter of days. It spreads sinewy tentacles rather than roots into the ground to search for its preferred food of earthworms. The Horklump is a favourite delicacy of gnomes but otherwise has no discernible use.

The Horklump will cover an average garden in a matter of days

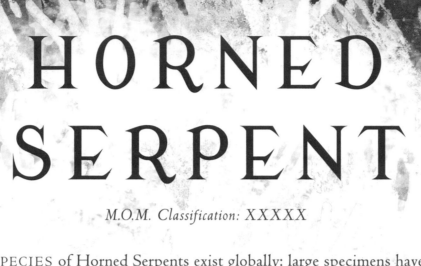

HORNED
SERPENT

M.O.M. Classification: XXXXX

SEVERAL SPECIES of Horned Serpents exist globally: large specimens have been caught in the Far East, while ancient bestiaries suggest that they were once native to Western Europe, where they have been hunted to extinction by wizards in search of potion ingredients. The largest and most diverse group of Horned Serpents still in existence is to be found in North America, of which the most famous and highly prized has a jewel in its forehead, which is reputed to give the power of invisibility and flight. A legend exists concerning the founder of Ilvermorny School of Witchcraft and Wizardry, Isolt Sayre, and a Horned Serpent. Sayre was reputed to be able to understand the serpent, which offered her shavings from its horn as the core of the first ever American-made wand. The Horned Serpent gives its name to one of the houses of Ilvermorny.

IMP

M.O.M. Classification: XX

THE IMP IS FOUND only in Britain and Ireland. It is sometimes confused with the pixie. They are of similar height (between six and eight inches), though the imp cannot fly as the pixie can, nor is it as vividly coloured (the imp is usually dark brown to black). It does, however, have a similar slapstick sense of humour. Its preferred terrain is damp and marshy, and it is often found near riverbanks, where it will amuse itself by pushing and tripping the unwary. Imps eat small insects and have breeding habits much like the fairies, though imps do not spin cocoons; the young are hatched fully formed at around one inch in length.

JARVEY

M.O.M. Classification: XXX

THE JARVEY is found in Britain, Ireland and North America. It resembles an overgrown ferret in most respects, except for the fact that it can talk. True conversation, however, is beyond the wit of the Jarvey, which tends to confine itself to short (and often rude) phrases in an almost constant stream. Jarveys live mostly below ground, where they pursue gnomes, though they will also eat moles, rats and voles.

JOBBERKNOLL

M.O.M. Classification: XX

THE JOBBERKNOLL (northern Europe and America) is a tiny blue, speckled bird which eats small insects. It makes no sound until the moment of its death, at which point it lets out a long scream made up of every sound it has ever heard, regurgitated backwards. Jobberknoll feathers are used in Truth Serums and Memory Potions.

A tiny blue, speckled bird which eats small insects

It resembles an overgrown ferret in most respects, except for the fact that it can talk

KAPPA

M.O.M. Classification: XXXX

THE KAPPA is a Japanese water demon that inhabits shallow ponds and rivers. Often said to look like a monkey with fish scales instead of fur, it has a hollow in the top of its head in which it carries water.

The Kappa feeds on human blood but may be persuaded not to harm a person if it is thrown a cucumber with that person's name carved into it. In confrontation, a wizard should trick the Kappa into bowing — if it does so, the water in the hollow of its head will run out, depriving it of all its strength.

KELPIE

M.O.M. Classification: XXXX

THIS BRITISH AND IRISH water demon can take various shapes, though it most often appears as a horse with bulrushes for a mane. Having lured the unwary on to its back, it will dive straight to the bottom of its river or lake and devour the rider, letting the entrails float to the surface. The correct means to overcome a kelpie is to get a bridle over its head with a Placement Charm, which renders it docile and unthreatening.

The world's largest kelpie is found in Loch Ness, Scotland. Its favourite form is that of a sea serpent (see below). International Confederation of Wizard observers realised that they were not dealing with a true serpent when they saw it turn into an otter on the approach of a team of Muggle investigators and then transform back into a serpent when the coast was clear.

73

KNARL

M.O.M. Classification: XXX

THE KNARL (northern Europe and America) is usually mistaken for a hedgehog by Muggles. The two species are indeed indistinguishable except for one important behavioural difference: if food is left out in the garden for a hedgehog, it will accept and enjoy the gift; if food is offered to a Knarl, on the other hand, it will assume that the householder is attempting to lure it into a trap and will savage that householder's garden plants or garden ornaments. Many a Muggle child has been accused of vandalism when an offended Knarl was the real culprit.

KNEAZLE

M.O.M. Classification: XXX

THE KNEAZLE was originally bred in Britain, though it is now exported worldwide. A small cat-like creature with flecked, speckled or spotted fur, outsize ears and a tail like a lion's, the Kneazle is intelligent, independent and occasionally aggressive, though if it takes a liking to a witch or wizard, it makes an excellent pet. The Kneazle has an uncanny ability to detect unsavoury or suspicious characters and can be relied upon to guide its owner safely home if they are lost. Kneazles have up to eight kittens in a litter and can interbreed with cats. Licences are required for ownership as (like Crups and Fwoopers) Kneazles are sufficiently unusual in appearance to attract Muggle interest.

LEPRECHAUN
(sometimes known as CLAURICORN)

M.O.M. Classification: XXX

MORE INTELLIGENT than the fairy and less malicious than the imp, the pixie or the Doxy, the leprechaun is nevertheless mischievous. Found only in Ireland, it achieves a height of up to six inches and is green in colour. It has been known to create crude clothing from leaves. Alone of the 'little people', leprechauns can speak, though they have never requested reclassification as 'beings'. The leprechaun bears live young and lives mostly in forest and woodland areas, though it enjoys attracting Muggle attention and as a consequence features almost as heavily as the fairy in Muggle literature for children. Leprechauns produce a realistic gold-like substance that vanishes after a few hours, to their great amusement. Leprechauns eat leaves and, despite their reputation as pranksters, are not known ever to have done lasting damage to a human.

Leprechauns produce a realistic gold-like substance that vanishes after a few hours

LETHIFOLD

(also known as LIVING SHROUD)

M.O.M. Classification: XXXXX

THE LETHIFOLD is a mercifully rare creature found solely in tropical climates. It resembles a black cloak perhaps half an inch thick (thicker if it has recently killed and digested a victim) which glides along the ground at night. The earliest account we have of a Lethifold was written by the wizard Flavius Belby, who was fortunate enough to survive a Lethifold attack in 1782 while holidaying in Papua New Guinea.

Near one o'clock in the morning, as I began at last to feel drowsy, I heard a soft rustling close by. Believing it to be nothing more than the leaves of the tree outside, I turned over in bed, with my back to the window, and caught sight of what appeared to be a shapeless black shadow sliding underneath my bedroom door. I lay motionless, trying sleepily to divine what was causing such a shadow in a room lit only by moonlight. Undoubtedly my stillness led the Lethifold to believe that its potential victim was sleeping.

To my horror, the shadow began to creep up the bed, and I felt its slight weight upon me.

It resembled nothing so much as a rippling black cape, the edges fluttering slightly as it slithered up the bed towards me. Paralysed with fear, I felt its clammy touch upon my chin before I sat bolt upright.

The thing attempted to smother me, sliding inexorably up my face, over my mouth and nostrils, but still I struggled, feeling it wrapping its coldness about me all the while. Unable to cry for assistance, I groped for my wand. Now dizzy as the thing sealed itself about my face, incapable of drawing breath, I concentrated with all my might upon the Stupefying Charm and then — as that failed to subdue the creature, though blasting a hole in my bedroom door — upon the Impediment Hex, which likewise availed me naught.

Still struggling madly, I rolled sideways and fell heavily to the floor, now entirely wrapped in the Lethifold.

I knew that I was about to lose consciousness completely as I suffocated. Desperately, I mustered up my last reserve of energy. Pointing my wand away from myself into the deadly folds of the creature, summoning the memory of the day I had been voted President of the local Gobstones Club, I performed the Patronus Charm.

Almost at once I felt fresh air upon my face. I looked up to see that deathly shadow being thrown into the air upon the horns of my Patronus. It flew across the room and slithered swiftly out of sight.

Flavius Belby
Papua New Guinea

As Belby so dramatically reveals, the Patronus is the only spell known to repel the Lethifold. Since it generally attacks the sleeping, though, its victims rarely have a chance to use any magic against it. Once its prey has been successfully suffocated, the Lethifold digests its food there and then in their bed. It then exits the house slightly thicker and fatter than before, leaving no trace of itself or its victim behind.[9]

9. The number of Lethifold victims is almost impossible to calculate since it leaves no clues to its presence behind it. Easier to calculate is the number of wizards who have, for their own unscrupulous purposes, pretended to have been killed by Lethifolds. The most recent instance of such duplicity occurred in 1973 when the wizard Janus Thickey vanished, leaving only a hastily written note on the bedside table reading 'oh no a Lethifold's got me I'm suffocating'. Convinced by the spotless and empty bed that such a creature had indeed killed Janus, his wife and children entered a period of strict mourning, which was rudely interrupted when Janus was discovered living five miles away with the landlady of the Green Dragon.

LOBALUG

M.O.M. Classification: XXX

THE LOBALUG IS found at the bottom of the North Sea. It is a simple creature, ten inches long, comprising a rubbery spout and a venom sac. When threatened, the Lobalug contracts its venom sac, blasting the attacker with poison. Merpeople use the Lobalug as a weapon and wizards have been known to extract its poison for use in potions, though this practice is strictly controlled.

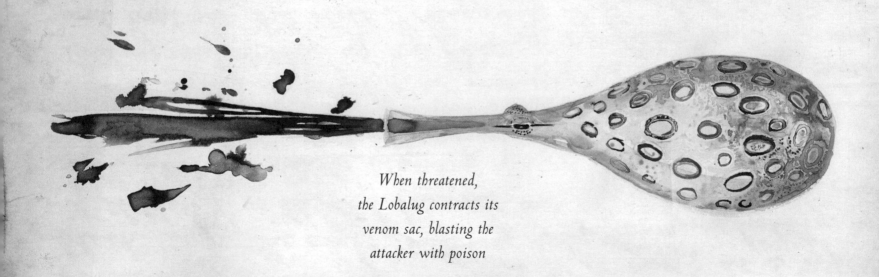

When threatened, the Lobalug contracts its venom sac, blasting the attacker with poison

*The Malaclaw's bite
has the unusual side
effect of making the victim
highly unlucky*

MACKLED MALACLAW

M.O.M. Classification: XXX

THE MALACLAW is a land-dwelling creature found mostly on rocky coastlines around Europe. Despite its passing resemblance to the lobster, it should on no account be eaten, as its flesh is unfit for human consumption and will result in a high fever and an unsightly greenish rash.

The Malaclaw can reach a length of twelve inches and is light grey with deep-green spots. It eats small crustaceans and will attempt to tackle larger prey. The Malaclaw's bite has the unusual side effect of making the victim highly unlucky for a period of up to a week after the injury. If you are bitten by a Malaclaw, all bets, wagers and speculative ventures should be cancelled, as they are sure to go against the victim.

MANTICORE

M.O.M. Classification: XXXXX

T HE MANTICORE is a highly dangerous Greek beast with the head of a man, the body of a lion and the tail of a scorpion. As dangerous as the Chimaera, and as rare, the Manticore is reputed to croon softly as it devours its prey. Manticore skin repels almost all known charms and the sting causes instant death.

The Manticore is reputed to croon softly as it devours its prey

MERPEOPLE

(also known as SIRENS, SELKIES, MERROWS)

M.O.M. Classification: XXXX[10]

MERPEOPLE EXIST throughout the world, though they vary in appearance almost as much as humans. Their habits and customs remain as mysterious as those of the centaur, though those wizards who have mastered the language of Mermish speak of highly organised communities varying in size according to habitat, and some have elaborately constructed dwellings. Like the centaurs, the merpeople have declined 'being' status in favour of a 'beast' classification (see Introduction).

The oldest recorded merpeople were known as sirens (Greece) and it is in warmer waters that we find the beautiful mermaids so frequently depicted in Muggle literature and painting. The selkies of Scotland and the merrows of Ireland are less beautiful, but they share that love of music which is common to all merpeople.

10. See classification footnote for centaur.

MOKE

M.O.M. Classification: XXX

THE MOKE IS A silver-green lizard reaching up to ten inches in length and is found throughout Britain and Ireland. It has the ability to shrink at will and has consequently never been noticed by Muggles.

Moke skin is highly prized among wizards for use as moneybags and purses, as the scaly material will contract at the approach of a stranger, just as its owner did; Moke-skin moneybags are therefore very difficult for thieves to locate.

MOONCALF

M.O.M. Classification: XX

THE MOONCALF is an intensely shy creature that emerges from its burrow only at the full moon. Its body is smooth and pale grey, it has bulging round eyes on top of its head and four spindly legs with enormous flat feet. Mooncalves perform complicated dances on their hind legs in isolated areas in the moonlight. These are believed to be a prelude to mating (and often leave intricate geometric patterns behind in wheat fields, to the great puzzlement of Muggles).

Watching Mooncalves dance by moonlight is a fascinating experience and often profitable, for if their silvery dung is collected before the sun rises and spread upon magical herb and flower beds, the plants will grow very fast and become extremely strong. Mooncalves are found worldwide.

MURTLAP

M.O.M. Classification: XXX

THE MURTLAP is a rat-like creature found in coastal areas of Britain. It has a growth upon its back resembling a sea anemone. When pickled and eaten, these Murtlap growths promote resistance to curses and jinxes, though an overdose may cause unsightly purple ear hair. Murtlaps eat crustaceans and the feet of anyone foolish enough to step on them.

Found in coastal areas of Britain

NIFFLER

M.O.M. Classification: XXX

THE NIFFLER IS a British beast. Fluffy, black and long-snouted, this burrowing creature has a predilection for anything glittery. Nifflers are often kept by goblins to burrow deep into the earth for treasure. Though the Niffler is gentle and even affectionate, it can be destructive to belongings and should never be kept in a house. Nifflers live in lairs up to twenty feet below the surface and produce six to eight young in a litter.

*This burrowing creature has
a predilection for anything glittery*

The Nogtail will creep into a sty and suckle an ordinary sow alongside her own young

NOGTAIL

M.O.M. Classification: XXX

NOGTAILS ARE demons found in rural areas right across Europe, Russia and America. They resemble stunted piglets with long legs, thick, stubby tails and narrow black eyes. The Nogtail will creep into a sty and suckle an ordinary sow alongside her own young. The longer the Nogtail is left undetected and the bigger it grows, the longer the blight on the farm into which it has entered.

The Nogtail is exceptionally fast and difficult to catch, though if chased beyond the boundaries of a farm by a pure white dog, it will never return. The Department for the Regulation and Control of Magical Creatures (Pest Sub-Division) keeps a dozen albino bloodhounds for this purpose.

NUNDU

M.O.M. Classification: XXXXX

THIS EAST AFRICAN beast is arguably the most dangerous in the world. A gigantic leopard that moves silently despite its size and whose breath causes disease virulent enough to eliminate entire villages, it has never yet been subdued by fewer than a hundred skilled wizards working together.

89

OCCAMY

M.O.M. Classification: XXXX

THE OCCAMY is found in the Far East and India. A plumed, two-legged winged creature with a serpentine body, the Occamy may reach a length of fifteen feet. It feeds mainly on rats and birds, though has been known to carry off monkeys. The Occamy is aggressive to all who approach it, particularly in defence of its eggs, whose shells are made of the purest, softest silver.

PHOENIX

M.O.M. Classification: XXXX[11]

THE PHOENIX IS a magnificent, swan-sized, scarlet bird with a long golden tail, beak and talons. It nests on mountain peaks and is found in Egypt, India and China. The phoenix lives to an immense age as it can regenerate, bursting into flames when its body begins to fail and rising again from the ashes as a chick. The phoenix is a gentle creature that has never been known to kill and eats only herbs. Like the Diricawl (see above), it can disappear and reappear at will. Phoenix song is magical: it is reputed to increase the courage of the pure of heart and to strike fear into the hearts of the impure. Phoenix tears have powerful healing properties.

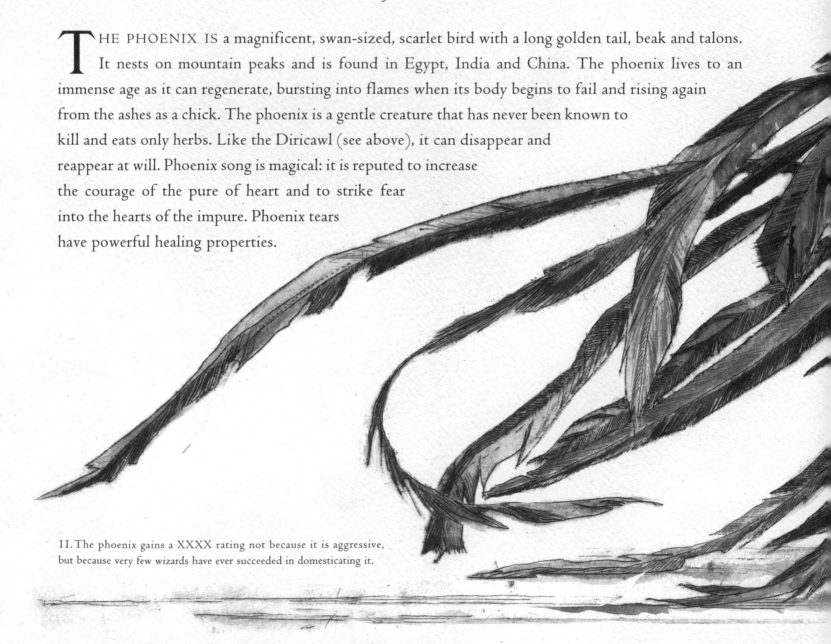

11. The phoenix gains a XXXX rating not because it is aggressive, but because very few wizards have ever succeeded in domesticating it.

PIXIE

M.O.M. Classification: XXX

THE PIXIE IS mostly found in Cornwall, England. Electric blue in colour, up to eight inches in height and very mischievous, the pixie delights in tricks and practical jokes of all descriptions. Although wingless, it can fly and has been known to seize unwary humans by the ears and deposit them at the tops of tall trees and buildings. Pixies produce a high-pitched jabbering intelligible only to other pixies. They bear live young.

PLIMPY

M.O.M. Classification: XXX

THE PLIMPY IS a spherical, mottled fish distinguished by its two long legs ending in webbed feet. It inhabits deep lakes, where it will prowl the bottom in search of food, preferring water snails. The Plimpy is not particularly dangerous, though it will nibble the feet and clothing of swimmers. It is considered a pest by merpeople, who deal with it by tying its rubbery legs in a knot; the Plimpy then drifts away, unable to steer, and cannot return until it has untied itself, which may take hours.

POGREBIN

M.O.M. Classification: XXX

THE POGREBIN IS a Russian demon, barely a foot tall, with a hairy body but a smooth, oversized grey head. When crouching, the Pogrebin resembles a shiny, round rock. Pogrebins are attracted to humans and enjoy tailing them, staying in their shadow and crouching quickly should the shadow's owner turn around. If a Pogrebin is allowed to tail a human for many hours, a sense of great futility will overcome its prey, who will eventually fall into a state of lethargy and despair. When the victim stops walking and sinks to their knees to weep at the pointlessness of it all, the Pogrebin will leap upon them and attempt to devour them. However, it is easy to repulse the Pogrebin with simple hexes or Stupefying Charms. Kicking has also been found effective.

PORLOCK

M.O.M. Classification: XX

THE PORLOCK IS a horse-guardian found in Dorset, England, and in Southern Ireland. Covered in shaggy fur, it has a large quantity of rough hair on its head and an exceptionally large nose. It walks on two cloven feet. The arms are small and end in four stubby fingers. Fully grown Porlocks are around two feet high and feed on grass.

The Porlock is shy and lives to guard horses. It may be found curled in the straw of stables or else sheltering in the midst of the herd it protects. Porlocks mistrust humans and always hide at their approach.

Porlock with small herd of horses. Corfe Castle

PUFFSKEIN

M.O.M. Classification: XX

THE PUFFSKEIN is found worldwide. Spherical in shape and covered in soft, custard-coloured fur, it is a docile creature that has no objection to being cuddled or thrown about. Easy to care for, it emits a low humming noise when contented. From time to time a very long, thin, pink tongue will emerge from the depths of the Puffskein and snake through the house searching for food. The Puffskein is a scavenger that will eat anything from leftovers to spiders, but it has a particular preference for sticking its tongue up the nose of sleeping wizards and eating their bogies. This tendency has made the Puffskein much beloved by wizarding children for many generations and it remains a highly popular wizarding pet.

From time to time a very long, thin, pink tongue will emerge from the depths of the Puffskein and snake through the house searching for food

QUINTAPED

(also known as HAIRY MACBOON)

M.O.M. Classification: XXXXX

THE QUINTAPED is a highly dangerous carnivorous beast with a particular taste for humans. Its low-slung body is covered with thick reddish-brown hair, as are its five legs, each of which ends in a clubfoot. The Quintaped is found only upon the Isle of Drear off the northernmost tip of Scotland. Drear has been made unplottable for this reason.

Legend has it that the Isle of Drear was once populated by two wizarding families, the McCliverts and the MacBoons. A drunken wizarding duel between Dugald, chief of the clan McClivert, and Quintius, head of the clan MacBoon, is supposed to have led to the death of Dugald. In retaliation, so the story has it, a gang of McCliverts surrounded the MacBoon dwellings one night and Transfigured each and every MacBoon into a monstrous five-legged creature. The McCliverts realised too late that the Transfigured MacBoons were infinitely more dangerous

The Isc

98

in this state (the MacBoons had the reputation for great ineptitude at magic). Moreover, the MacBoons resisted every attempt to turn them back into human form. The monsters killed every last one of the McCliverts until no human remained on the island. It was only then that the MacBoon monsters realised that in the absence of anyone to wield a wand, they would be forced to remain as they were for evermore.

Whether this tale is true or not will never be known. Certainly there are no surviving McCliverts or MacBoons to tell us what happened to their ancestors. The Quintapeds cannot talk and have strenuously resisted every attempt by the Department for the Regulation and Control of Magical Creatures to capture a specimen and try to Untransfigure it, so we must assume that if they are indeed, as their nickname suggests, Hairy MacBoons, they are quite happy to live out their days as beasts.

Drear

One spies the hairy monsters from afar and daresn't approach too close to the shore

RAMORA

M.O.M. Classification: XX

THE RAMORA IS a silver fish found in the Indian Ocean. Powerfully magical, it can anchor ships and is a guardian of seafarers. The Ramora is highly valued by the International Confederation of Wizards, which has set many laws in place to protect the Ramora from wizard poachers.

Powerfully magical,
it can anchor ships and is
a guardian of seafarers

RED CAP

M.O.M. Classification: XXX

THESE DWARF-LIKE creatures live in holes on old battlegrounds or wherever human blood has been spilled. Although easily repelled by charms and hexes, they are very dangerous to solitary Muggles, whom they will attempt to bludgeon to death on dark nights. Red Caps are most prevalent in northern Europe.

RE'EM

M.O.M. Classification: XXXX

EXTREMELY RARE giant oxen with golden hides, the Re'em are found both in the wilds of North America and the Far East. Re'em blood gives the drinker immense strength, though the difficulty in procuring it means that supplies are negligible and rarely for sale on the open market.

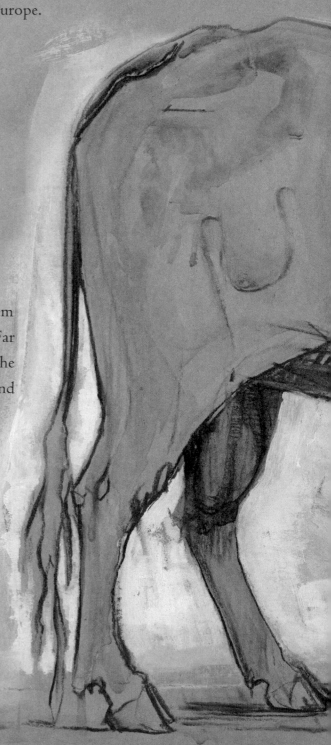

103

RUNESPOOR

M.O.M. Classification: XXXX

THE RUNESPOOR originated in the small African country of Burkina Faso. A three-headed serpent, the Runespoor commonly reaches a length of six or seven feet. Livid orange with black stripes, the Runespoor is only too easy to spot, so the Ministry of Magic in Burkina Faso has designated certain forests unplottable for the Runespoor's sole use.

The Runespoor, though not in itself a particularly vicious beast, was once a favourite pet of Dark wizards, no doubt because of its striking and intimidating appearance. It is to the writings of Parselmouths who have kept and conversed with these serpents that we owe our understanding of their curious habits. It transpires from their records that each of the Runespoor's heads serves a different purpose. The left head (as seen by the wizard facing the Runespoor) is the planner. It decides where the Runespoor is to go and what it is to do next. The middle head is the dreamer (Runespoors may remain stationary for days at a time, lost in glorious visions and imaginings). The right head is the critic and will evaluate the efforts of the left and middle heads with a continual irritable hissing. The right head's fangs are extremely venomous. The Runespoor rarely reaches a great age, as the heads tend to attack each other. It is common to see a Runespoor with the right head missing, the other two heads having banded together to bite it off.

The Runespoor produces eggs through its mouths, the only known magical beast so to do. These eggs are of immense value in the production of potions to stimulate mental agility. A black market in Runespoor eggs and in the serpents themselves has flourished for several centuries.

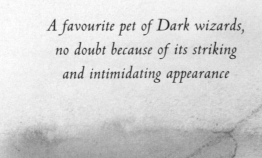

*A favourite pet of Dark wizards,
no doubt because of its striking
and intimidating appearance*

SALAMANDER

M.O.M. Classification: XXX

THE SALAMANDER is a small fire-dwelling lizard that feeds on flame. Brilliant white, it appears blue or scarlet depending upon the heat of the fire in which it makes its appearance.

Salamanders can survive up to six hours outside a fire if regularly fed pepper. They will live only as long as the fire from which they sprang burns. Salamander blood has powerful curative and restorative properties.

SEA SERPENT

M.O.M. Classification: XXX

SEA SERPENTS are found in the Atlantic, Pacific and Mediterranean seas. Though alarming in appearance, sea serpents are not known ever to have killed any human, despite hysterical Muggle accounts of their ferocious behaviour. Reaching lengths of up to a hundred feet, the sea serpent has a horse-like head and a long snake-like body that rises in humps out of the sea.

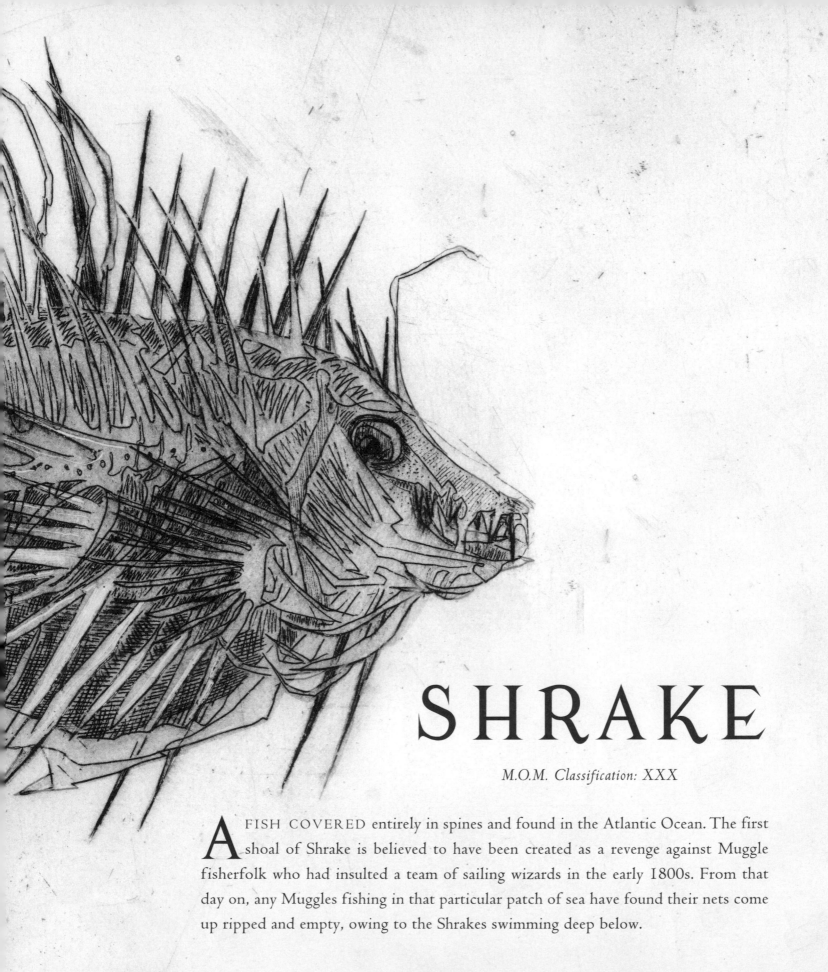

SHRAKE

M.O.M. Classification: XXX

A FISH COVERED entirely in spines and found in the Atlantic Ocean. The first shoal of Shrake is believed to have been created as a revenge against Muggle fisherfolk who had insulted a team of sailing wizards in the early 1800s. From that day on, any Muggles fishing in that particular patch of sea have found their nets come up ripped and empty, owing to the Shrakes swimming deep below.

*Possesses fangs of
serrated steel with which
it slices through its prey*

110

SNALLYGASTER

M.O.M. Classification: XXXX

NATIVE TO NORTH AMERICA, the part-bird, part-reptile Snallygaster was once believed to be a kind of dragon, but is now known to be a distant relative of the Occamy. It cannot breathe fire, but possesses fangs of serrated steel with which it slices through its prey. The Snallygaster has frequently endangered the International Statute of Secrecy. Its natural curiosity, coupled with a bulletproof hide, renders it difficult to scare away and the Snallygaster has found its way into Muggle newspapers with such frequency that it sometimes ties with the Loch Ness Monster for 'Most Publicity-Hungry Beast'. Since 1949, a dedicated Snallygaster Protection League has been stationed permanently in Maryland to Obliviate Muggles who see it.

SNIDGET

M.O.M. Classification: XXXX[12]

THE GOLDEN SNIDGET is an extremely rare, protected species of bird. Completely round, with a very long, thin beak and glistening, jewel-like red eyes, the Golden Snidget is an extremely fast flier that can change direction with uncanny speed and skill, owing to the rotational joints of its wings.

The Golden Snidget's feathers and eyes are so highly prized that it was at one time in danger of being hunted to extinction by wizards. The danger was recognised in time and the species protected, the most notable factor being the substitution of the Golden Snitch for the Snidget in the game of Quidditch.[13] Snidget sanctuaries exist worldwide.

12. The Golden Snidget gains a XXXX rating not because it is dangerous but because severe penalties are attached to its capture or injury.

13. Anyone interested in the role played by the Golden Snidget in the development of the game of Quidditch is advised to consult *Quidditch Through the Ages* by Kennilworthy Whisp (Whizz Hard Books, 1952).

113

SPHINX

M.O.M. Classification: XXXX

THE EGYPTIAN SPHINX has a human head on a lion's body. For over a thousand years it has been used by witches and wizards to guard valuables and secret hideaways. Highly intelligent, the sphinx delights in puzzles and riddles. It is usually dangerous only when what it is guarding is threatened.

STREELER

M.O.M. Classification: XXX

THE STREELER is a giant snail that changes colour on an hourly basis and deposits behind it a trail so venomous that it shrivels and burns all vegetation over which it passes. The Streeler is native to several African countries, though it has been successfully raised by wizards in Europe, Asia and the Americas. It is kept as a pet by those who enjoy its kaleidoscopic colour changes, and its venom is one of the few substances known to kill Horklumps.

A trail so venomous that it shrivels and burns all vegetation over which it passes

TEBO

M.O.M. Classification: XXXX

THE TEBO is an ash-coloured warthog found in Congo and Zaire. It has the power of invisibility, making it difficult to evade or catch, and is very dangerous. Tebo hide is highly prized by wizards for protective shields and clothing.

120

THUNDERBIRD

M.O.M. Classification: XXXX

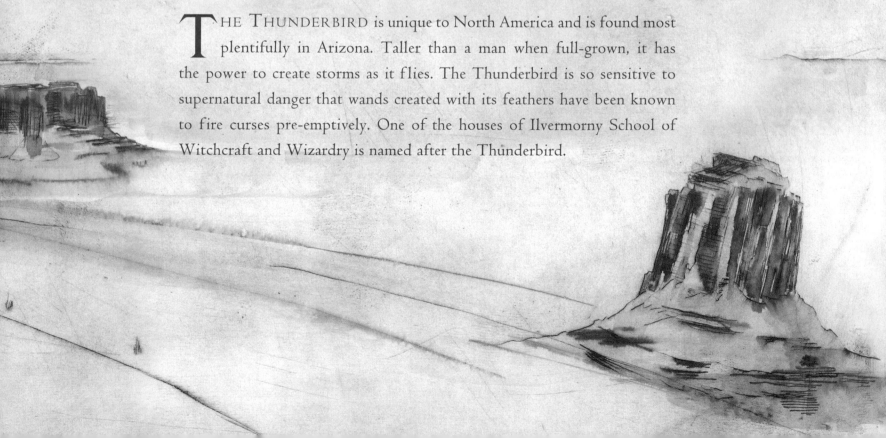

THE THUNDERBIRD is unique to North America and is found most plentifully in Arizona. Taller than a man when full-grown, it has the power to create storms as it flies. The Thunderbird is so sensitive to supernatural danger that wands created with its feathers have been known to fire curses pre-emptively. One of the houses of Ilvermorny School of Witchcraft and Wizardry is named after the Thunderbird.

TROLL

M.O.M. Classification: XXXX

THE TROLL is a fearsome creature up to twelve feet tall and weighing over a tonne. Notable for its equally prodigious strength and stupidity, the troll is often violent and unpredictable. Trolls originated in Scandinavia but these days they may be found in Britain, Ireland and other areas of northern Europe.

Trolls generally converse in grunts that appear to constitute a crude language, though some have been known to understand and even to speak a few simple human words. The more intelligent of the species have been trained as guardians.

There are three types of troll: mountain, forest and river. The mountain troll is the largest and most vicious. It is bald, with a pale-grey skin. The forest troll has a pale-green skin and some specimens have hair, which is green or brown, thin and straggly. The river troll has short horns and may be hairy. It has a purplish skin and is often found lurking beneath bridges. Trolls eat raw flesh and are not fussy in their prey, which ranges from wild animals to humans.

UNICORN

M.O.M. Classification: XXXX[14]

THE UNICORN is a beautiful beast found throughout the forests of northern Europe. It is a pure white, horned horse when fully grown, though the foals are initially golden and turn silver before achieving maturity. The unicorn's horn, blood and hair all have highly magical properties.[15] It generally avoids human contact, is more likely to allow a witch to approach it than a wizard, and is so fleet of foot that it is very difficult to capture.

14. See footnote on centaur classification.
15. The unicorn, like the fairy, has received an excellent Muggle press — in this case justified.

124

125

WAMPUS CAT

M.O.M. Classification: XXXXX

SOMEWHAT RESEMBLING the mundane mountain lion or cougar in size and appearance, the Wampus Cat is native to Appalachia. It can walk on its hind legs, outrun arrows, and its yellow eyes are reputed to have the power of both hypnosis and Legilimency. The Cherokee have most extensively studied the Wampus Cat, with whom they share their native region, and only they have ever succeeded in procuring Wampus Cat hair for use as a wand core. In 1832, wizard Abel Treetops of Cincinnati claimed to have patented a method of taming Wampus Cats for use as guards over wizarding houses. Treetops was exposed as a fraud when MACUSA raided his home and found him putting Engorgement Charms on Kneazles. One of the houses of the North American wizarding school, Ilvermorny, is named after the Wampus Cat.

128

WEREWOLF

M.O.M. Classification: XXXXX[16]

THE WEREWOLF is found worldwide, though it is believed to have originated in northern Europe. Humans turn into werewolves only when bitten. There is no known cure, though recent developments in potion-making have to a great extent alleviated the worst symptoms. Once a month, at the full moon, the otherwise sane and normal wizard or Muggle afflicted transforms into a murderous beast. Almost uniquely among fantastic creatures, the werewolf actively seeks humans in preference to any other kind of prey.

16. This classification refers, of course, to the werewolf in its transformed state. When there is no full moon, the werewolf is as harmless as any other human. For a heart-rending account of one wizard's battle with lycanthropy, see the classic *Hairy Snout, Human Heart* by an anonymous author (Whizz Hard Books, 1975).

130

WINGED
HORSE

M.O.M. Classification: XX–XXXX

WINGED HORSES exist worldwide. There are many different breeds, including the Abraxan (immensely powerful giant palominos), the Aethonan (chestnut, popular in Britain and Ireland), the Granian (grey and particularly fast) and the rare Thestral (black, possessed of the power of invisibility and considered unlucky by many wizards). As with the Hippogriff, the owner of a winged horse is required to perform a Disillusionment Charm upon it at regular intervals (see Introduction).

YETI

(also known as BIGFOOT, the ABOMINABLE SNOWMAN)

M.O.M. Classification: XXXX

A NATIVE OF TIBET, the yeti is believed to be related to the troll, though no one has yet got close enough to conduct the necessary tests. Up to fifteen feet in height, it is covered head to foot in purest white hair. The yeti devours anything that strays into its path, though it fears fire and may be repulsed by skilled wizards.

The illustrator would like to thank Alison Eldred;
Ray Lowden, Hope, Sima and Cora from the Kielder Water Birds of Prey Centre;
Belle Drury, Keeper of Rhinos; Hellen Pethers from the Natural History Museum;
Chain Bridge Honey Farm; John and Freddy Hamblin; Chandrakant Patel; Rose and Tony Dobbin;
Charlie Poulsen and Pauline Burbidge; Kathleen Jamie; Vincent Lomenech;
and Gabhran, Elzéard and Arthos.

Olivia Lomenech Gill

List of Beasts

Acromantula................2
Ashwinder................4
Augurey................4

Basilisk................6
Billywig................8
Bowtruckle................9
Bundimun................10

Centaur................12
Chimaera................14
Chizpurfle................16
Clabbert................18
Crup................19

Demiguise................20
Diricawl................22
Doxy................23
Dragon................24
    Antipodean Opaleye
    Chinese Fireball
    Common Welsh Green
    Hebridean Black
    Hungarian Horntail
    Norwegian Ridgeback
    Peruvian Vipertooth
    Romanian Longhorn
    Swedish Short-Snout
    Ukrainian Ironbelly
Dugbog................38

Erkling................40
Erumpent................42

Fairy................44
Fire Crab................44
Flobberworm................45
Fwooper................45

Ghoul................46
Glumbumble................48
Gnome................49
Graphorn................50
Griffin................52
Grindylow................54

Hidebehind................56
Hippocampus................58
Hippogriff................60
Hodag................62
Horklump................64
Horned Serpent................66

Imp................68

Jarvey................70
Jobberknoll................70

Kappa................72
Kelpie................72
Knarl................74
Kneazle................74

Leprechaun................75
Lethifold................76
Lobalug................79

Mackled Malaclaw................80
Manticore................81
Merpeople................82
Moke................84
Mooncalf................84
Murtlap................85

Niffler................86
Nogtail................87
Nundu................88

Occamy................90

Phoenix................92
Pixie................94
Plimpy................94
Pogrebin................95
Porlock................95
Puffskein................96

Quintaped................98

Ramora................100
Red Cap................102
Re'em................102
Runespoor................104

Salamander................106
Sea Serpent................107
Shrake................108
Snallygaster................110
Snidget................112
Sphinx................114
Streeler................116

Tebo................118
Thunderbird................120
Troll................122

Unicorn................124

Wampus Cat................126
Werewolf................128
Winged Horse................130

Yeti................132

J.K. Rowling

J.K. Rowling is the author of the record-breaking, multi-award-winning Harry Potter novels. Loved by fans around the world, the series has sold over 450 million copies, been translated into 79 languages, and made into eight blockbuster films. She has written three companion volumes in aid of charity: *Quidditch Through the Ages* and *Fantastic Beasts and Where to Find Them* (which were written in aid of Comic Relief and now support both Comic Relief and Lumos), and *The Tales of Beedle the Bard* (in aid of Lumos), as well as a screenplay inspired by *Fantastic Beasts and Where to Find Them*. She has also collaborated on a stage play, *Harry Potter and the Cursed Child Parts One and Two*, which opened in London's West End in the summer of 2016. In 2012, J.K. Rowling's digital company Pottermore was launched, where fans can enjoy her new writing and immerse themselves deeper in the wizarding world. She has received many awards and honours, including an OBE for services to children's literature, France's Légion d'honneur and the Hans Christian Andersen Award.

Olivia Lomenech Gill

Olivia Lomenech Gill has a first class degree in Theatre from the University of Hull and an MA in Printmaking from Camberwell College of Arts. She has built her career as a professional fine artist and has been exhibited at all the major London art fairs. Olivia's first professional illustration commission, *Where My Wellies Take Me*, written by Clare and Michael Morpurgo, was shortlisted for the Kate Greenaway Medal and won the English Association Picture Book Award. Olivia lives and works in north Northumberland in a timber studio she built by hand with her husband, a paper conservator. They also have a workshop in a nearby village, which houses Olivia's three-tonne printing press.

Since 2001, *Quidditch Through the Ages* and *Fantastic Beasts and Where to Find Them* have raised nearly £20 million for Comic Relief – a magic amount of money that is already hard at work changing lives.

Money raised through the sale of this new edition will be invested in children and young people around the world, preparing them to be ready for the future – to be safe, healthy, educated and empowered. We are particularly interested in helping those children who start their lives in the most difficult circumstances, where there is conflict, violence, neglect or abuse.

Thank you for your support. To find out more about Comic Relief go to comicrelief.com, follow us on Twitter (@comicrelief) or like us on Facebook!

There are eight million children living in orphanages worldwide – even though eighty per cent of them are not orphans.

Most children are institutionalised because their parents are poor and cannot adequately provide for them. And while many institutions are established or supported with good intentions, more than eighty years of research proves that raising children in orphanages harms their health and development, increases their exposure to abuse and trafficking and seriously reduces their chances of a happy, healthy future.

Put simply, children need families, not orphanages.

Lumos, a charity founded by J.K. Rowling, is named after the light-giving spell from Harry Potter that brings light to the darkest of places. At Lumos that is exactly what we do. We reveal the children hidden away in institutions and transform systems of care globally so that all children have the families they need and the futures they deserve.

Thank you for buying this book. If you would like to join J.K. Rowling and Lumos as part of our global movement for change you can find out how to get involved at wearelumos.org, @lumos and Facebook.